MYSTIC KNIGHT

LADY BLADE
BOOK THREE

CLARA WILS

Gryphon's Gate Publishing

Mystic Knight

Gryphon's Gate Publishing

550 King St. N.

PO Box 42088 Conestoga

Waterloo, ON

N2L 6K5

Print ISBN: 978-1-990587-59-7

CHAPTER 1

Tisera

I had to stop Dantoine!

He was hurting my guys as a way of torturing me. He'd started by sinking a knife into Kel's stomach with the intent of disemboweling him. But he'd only just begun, and if I could free myself of my rope bindings, perhaps I could stop him.

To that end, I'd pulled a heavy nail from the wooden beam behind me and I'd been using it to loosen my bonds. Yet, my hands were a bloody mess from pulling that nail out and I kept losing my grip on the iron spike.

And even if I got free, Dantoine had used knives to disable me: one sunk into my stomach and one in each thigh.

Still, I had to do something.

I redoubled my efforts to free myself, thrusting the

nail through the ropes so hard it punctured my other hand. I didn't care, pulling it back a little I viciously sawed at the ropes, while pulling my wrists apart. My arms burned where the ropes dug in, but I felt the bonds loosen. Then they fell away entirely.

My heart surged with hope. I'd done it!

I reached around quickly, pulling the knife from my gut and flinging it at Dantoine.

Blood sprayed from my torn-up hands as I threw the knife, a ghastly sight. And with blood-slicked, half-numb fingers, I hadn't thrown well. The knife hit Dantoine's shoulder instead of my intended target... his eye.

Dantoine's eyes went wide even as I pulled one of the knives out of my thigh and threw again.

But he was a trained warrior and had reacted quickly after my first throw. He dodged the second throw and since he already had a knife in hand, the one he'd been using to torture Kel, he flung it at me. He was fresh, mostly unharmed, and far more accurate than I. His knife hit high in my chest, to the right side of center, and sank in deep.

The intense, piercing pain caused me to fall back. I screamed, in agony and frustration... or I would have. When I opened my mouth, all that came out was a long gasping wheeze. Then my breath caught and my chest spasmed, burning. Some — far more analytical — part of my mind knew the blade had hit a lung. I'd seen it before, in others, on the battlefield.

Not good.

But I wasn't dead yet.

Forcing myself back up, I pulled the blade in my other

thigh free and kept it in hand as Dantoine plucked the knife out of his shoulder and launched himself at me. I couldn't do much, I was weak, and my hands were nearly numb. I simply stabbed at him as he landed next to me. I hit his gut and the force of his arrival drove the knife in so deep my hand followed it into the wound.

He'd meant to slash my throat, but my stab had jarred him just enough that his blade slid over my chin instead. His knife cut deep into my jawbone, then raked up over my cheek and up across my ear and into my hair. Making the most of my hit and his miss, I slashed wildly with the knife in his gut, driving it up into his vital organs. Then I released it and grabbed a handful of his insides pulling them out.

He screamed, looking down, horrified, at his bowels in my hand. Then, even as his eyes began to glass over, he stabbed down with his knife for one final strike.

I didn't have much strength left, but I flung my other arm up to block. The knife drove through my limb and down into my chest, pinning my arm to me, just above my left breast. That would have been a killing blow, but I'd stopped it.

I released his guts and drove two fingers up into his one eye... as hard as I could.

He flinched and fell back, releasing the knife in my arm and flailing wildly. That would only cause the knife I'd left inside him to do more damage and with the far-too-large hole in his gut already he was done for.

He thrashed about, as blood spurted from him and gore fell out. Then... his movements stilled to a series of twitches. I didn't know if he was dead or still dying, but that didn't matter. I needed to do something about my own condition... now!

Having removed the three knives from my gut and thighs, blood from those wounds flowed freely. That, along with my new wounds, meant I didn't have long before I'd be as limp and twitching as Dantoine.

I needed to get to Daz and wake him, so he could heal me.

My legs were still bound, yet even if I freed them, I'd not be able to walk with the wounds in my legs. Hells, I doubted I'd even be able to crawl very far, given how weak I was.

I flopped onto my stomach and began to slowly — tortuously slowly, since I was a bloody mess — drag myself across the floor to where my guys lay.

I still had two knives in my chest. I dared not remove them.

I might be able to take out the knife pinning my left arm to my chest. Using both hands would certainly make crawling easier, but I'd also lose more blood, which I couldn't afford.

As for the knife which had punctured my lung, removing it would only make matters worse. Still, I could barely catch my breath as I scraped myself over that packed earth floor.

Darkness grasped at the edges of my vision. A blurry haze filtered over everything. The dozen or so feet I needed to travel seemed like miles.

Inch by slow, precious inch, I clawed my way across the floor, leaving a trail of blood behind me. When I passed by Dantoine's face, I saw life in his eyes. He tried to speak, but only burbled up blood, choking on it. Then slowly the light faded from his eyes.

Good riddance.

I continued my desperate crawl, flinging my arm out to pull myself another aching inch.

I lost all sense of time. A minute became hours as I clung to consciousness, defiant of death and pressing forward.

Inch.

...

By.

...

Inch.

Then, when I threw my arm out ahead of me to pull me forward yet once more... I hit something.

Rousing from the dazed semi-consciousness I'd fallen into, I looked up to see Daz. I'd touched his arm.

"Daz!" I tried to call, to whisper, to make any sound, but all that came out was a long wheeze, which shot pains through my chest. So, since I couldn't speak, I slapped his arm repeatedly, as hard as I could, in hopes that might rouse him.

But he didn't move.

I didn't have much time left. A heavy, numbing cold had seized my legs. I couldn't feel my fingers. My frantic swatting of Daz slowed and stopped as my arms became dead weights. It was all I could do to simply remain conscious now.

Please Daz! Wake up! Please. I'd resorted to yelling in my thoughts, in the vain hope that somehow his mystic Phorasti senses would pick that up.

Tears leaked out of my eyes. I didn't want to die like this, having defeated that sadistic man and so close to someone who could help me.

My dazed mind clung to the horrible thought that Daz might wake to find me so close, but dead. When he saw that I'd struggled to get to him, but he'd not been able to help me, it would shatter his caring soul.

So, I fought. I fought just to keep breathing. I fought with every beat of my heart. I fought to keep my eyes open, even once darkness had nearly taken my vision and all I could see was a small patch of floor below me. And when my eyes closed and breathing became harder, I fought in my mind. I yelled at myself to live, to survive, that I'd been through worse — which I hadn't — and I could make it through this.

Light faded.

I dwelled in darkness.

An all-encompassing void dragged me away from my senses. I'd first lost my sense of touch. Then I'd lost my sight, then hearing. All I had now was smell, the acrid, bitter coppery tang of blood all around me. That was all I could smell, that and worse. But even that started drifting away. When that was gone, some part of me knew I'd not be able to return to myself. I'd be dead.

Then... curiously... I heard something.

Not the sound of my own labored breath. Not the scrape or creak of someone walking above me. Not a voice. No sound of the outside world.

I heard...

...music...

...slowly surrounding me in this vast emptiness.

It began as a hymn, solemn and stoic, so quiet I could barely hear it. Then it strengthened, coming into focus.

Then came... singing? No words, just beautiful voices raised to accompany the hymn.

It captured my soul, an exquisite song.

And slowly, a second melody joined the first: a soft and soothing lullaby. And somehow, this new chorus — high and clear and vibrant — worked in concert with the hymn, adding to it, not discordant.

Then a low beat — like that of my own heart, steady and sure — blended with this dual refrain.

And when it came together it forged an anthem, powerful and stirring.

I didn't know what this music could be. Perhaps such beautiful music played for everyone when they died, or perhaps this was just my personal experience of dying and passing into the hands of the gods? If so, it was beautiful and powerful... which made sense.

Yet, I couldn't go.

I couldn't die.

I needed to save Pearlia from whatever Veora had planned.

Though, that commitment paled in comparison with the need to save my men. They were my life, my meaning, my reason for living. Without them...

Leo, Kel, Daz! I love you all. I need you.

Hear me! Heal me! Save me! Please... PLEASE!

And with that cry, the song within me blossomed, soaring through a key change to a stunning and powerful crescendo.

The last notes echoed within my soul...

Then slowly faded, till I was left with silence.
Falling into darkness...
...further from warmth...
...and light...
... and love.

CHAPTER 2

D<small>AZAR</small>

T<small>HE CRY CAME CLEARLY AND POWERFULLY TO MY MIND</small>:
Hear me! Heal me! Save me! Please... PLEASE!

I knew that voice like I knew my own.

Tisi.

She needed my help.

Behind her words came a flood of Phora so powerful it filled my soul. It washed over me, overwhelming me, a tidal wave of colors, blended together into perfect white. I didn't know how, but Tisi had connected to me and...

...healed me.

A soothing warmth spread through me. My aches and pains faded.

I'd been unable to move, and only semi-aware, after that woman had overpowered me with her Ikiosti powers. The woman who looked like Tisi but wasn't. I'd tried to stop her, tried to resist her, but I'd been too weak, too drained. Then, a man had come and beaten me, broken me.

After that... I'd lingered in a place of pain and fevered dreams.

Until now.

The pain vanished.

The fever lifted.

I felt more at peace and stronger than I had in a long time. I drew in a long, revivifying breath.

My eyes fluttered open and I looked up at the underside of a wooden floor... uncertain where I was.

"Tisi?" I whispered.

No response.

I rose slowly, carefully. The brute who'd roughed me up had shattered my back during his vicious beating. But... I was able to sit up well enough: no injuries, no pain. I should have been broken, crippled, covered in cuts and bruises, my face a swollen mess, but when I raised a hand to check, I felt only smooth skin.

I was completely healed... somehow.

And full of life and energy. I'd been drained of my powers — from spending an entire day showing the queen what I could do, then using what little remained to resist that Ikiosti — but now a renewed potency surged through me.

A miracle.

I couldn't explain this... well, there was one explanation, that I'd been unconscious and laid up for weeks or months and somehow healed naturally on my own, but I got the feeling only a short time had passed. So, what had happened?

Tisi was involved. I'd heard her voice before the colors had moved over and through me. It made no sense. It was like some incredibly powerful Phorasti had healed me, but...

"Tisi?" I asked again, only now bothering to look around. Leo and Kel roused, slowly rising from where they lay. We were in a dim cellar. There had been a fight here. The man who'd beaten me was dead across the room and...

Next to me lay the bloody form of Tisi, knives protruding from her, blood rushing out of her from so many wounds.

"No!" I screamed and instantly summoned my powers. I used green to connect with her, but instantly I sensed that closing her wounds wouldn't be enough.

She was dead, for all intents and purposes. Her heart had stopped, her spirit fading.

But... she wasn't completely gone.

I summoned white and violet to connect our souls and found the last shred of her spirit, clinging to life. I reached out to that and held on, keeping Tisi from slipping away.

I'd kept her from dying, but bringing her back...

The trouble with Phorasti healing was that it was exponential, not linear. Healing ten injuries took a hundred times the power of just one. Bringing someone back from the brink of death would kill the healer. I couldn't heal her fully. It was impossible. I didn't have that much power.

I carefully rolled her over and drew out the knives still sticking out of her as I surged green to close the worst of her wounds, but only just. Healing any more would drain me too much for what was to come. Yet I needed to do that much or restoring her to life would only cause more blood to flow out of her.

To restart her heart, I pounded red over and over into her chest, until the vital organ lurched to life, beating — ever so weakly — once more. Then I put everything I could, summoning white for power and violet for spirit to pull her fading soul back into her near-to-lifeless body. I hoped it would be enough... because that was all I could do.

I'd drained myself yet again. The world spun. My body went limp. I fell but was caught by strong arms.

Kel held me.

"Is she alive?" he asked, concern on his face and in his voice.

I found it vaguely disturbing that he was more worried about Tisi than me, but then... I'd probably be the same.

I nodded.

My voice quavered when I spoke. "She was dead when I found her, or as dead as a person can be and still return. She'll live, but... her spirit was so distant. I don't know if I did enough to return it to her." I'd tried to drag her back from death but didn't know if I'd done enough. "The rest is up to her."

Kel nodded. "And you?" he asked.

I smiled. So, he *was* concerned for me too, but... secondarily. At least his priorities were straight.

"I'll be well enough, just drained." *Again.*

Tisi groaned and it was the most glorious sound I'd ever heard as it meant she was reviving.

"She can't move too much, or her wounds will reopen," I said to the other two men. Kel set me down carefully, then went to her. Leo joined him.

The prince leaned over Tisi, holding her gently. "Be still," he whispered to her as her eyes fluttered open.

She smiled. "Leo?" Her voice was rough, harsh and raw. "I thought... Daz...?"

"He's here, he healed you," Leo breathed, as if even a raised voice might hurt her.

She smiled but seemed so very weak, not fully with us yet, dazed and delirious.

"And all of you as well? Good. I... I need to..." She tried to rise but could barely move. Leo helped her, moving her carefully to a reclined position in his lap.

"Be still. I have you. Don't move, you're still healing." Leo's voice was soft and soothing.

"No... I... Veora... at... the palace... Stop her." She was fading now, going limp. She'd used all her energy to convey that message. Her eyes fluttered closed as unconsciousness took her. Leo laid her down carefully.

"Veora..." Kel hissed, as his face colored with shame.

Was that her name?

"Is she the one who lured us here? The woman who looked like Tisi but wasn't? If so, she's an Ikiosti, a Phorasti like me but her power manifests through sound."

Kel looked away, his color rising. "She... she made us..."

Yes. We'd all been overcome with arousal and the

result had been an embarrassment of colossal proportions.

Kel continued, voice hard. "Yes, that was Veora." It sounded like he didn't want to remember at all. I could understand that. What she'd made us do... not only had it been horribly mortifying and shameful, but it had left us all so very weak. I'd been violated, and I guessed Kel felt the same.

"That's behind us now," Leo said. His cheeks were tinged with a scandalized blush as well. "Tisi used all her strength to warn us of Veora. We need to heed that and do something." Leo turned to me. "Can you walk?"

I'd worn myself out again. I didn't even know if I'd be able to rise. I shrugged.

Kel, good man that he was, helped me up slowly. I could stand on my own and shuffle around, but I wouldn't move quickly. Kel passed me to Leo, who became my crutch, helping me walk. Then Kel picked up Tisi and carried her cradled in his arms.

Before we left, we did a quick raid of the house. Tisi was next to naked, her dress torn down the front. The rest of us were a mess from Veora's... stimulation. Not a good look.

We stole some clothes and dressed quickly. Kel had to go bare-chested since nothing here fit his large frame. We put Tisi in one of Veora's dresses, something easy to slip on, a tubular affair with a tie around the waist and another tie behind the neck, leaving most of the back exposed. We also found a stash of weapons and armed ourselves.

Then we made all haste for the palace.

CHAPTER 3

Leonin

It was late, and we were an odd-looking troop, armed to the teeth. So, I wasn't surprised that the gate guards stopped us.

The main gates were closed, but people could still get in and out through the wicket gate: a smaller, single-person door built into the larger gate. But you had to have special dispensation to get through the wicket... which we didn't have.

We were questioned, while we yelled at them that we didn't have time for this. Then the captain of the gate showed up and luckily recognized me, but this only caused more confusion.

"Your Highness?" the captain asked, clearly perplexed. "Did you leave the city again?"

"Leave the city? Again? What do you mean?" I was tired and confused.

The captain eyed me, more and more suspicious. "You came through here not long ago... looking a far sight more regal than you do now. You also mentioned that if anyone else arrived looking like you, that they were an imposter and to be detained."

That was impossible.

"Fuck," Daz breathed next to me. He wasn't quite dead weight leaning on me but helping him along had taken a lot out of me. I really needed to take Tisi's advice and get stronger.

"What?" I asked Daz.

"If Veora could look like Tisi, then she could probably look like one of us."

"Fuck," I repeated, understanding now.

"If you wouldn't mind coming with me... *Your Highness*." The captain clearly didn't believe us. "I'm sure we can clear this up." He looked over at Kel with Tisi in his arms. "And who is the woman? Is she injured?" From the man's tone, it was clear he thought we'd been the ones who'd injured her.

This was not going well for us. However... if we were going to be questioned, that would happen on the other side of the gate. They'd have to let us in.

"She is hurt, yes, but we didn't do that. We are trying to get her some help," I said. "And we will not fight you, captain, we will go with you willingly."

"We will?" Kel said surprised.

"We will," I insisted.

He shrugged.

"I'm glad to hear that," the captain said. "This way

please." He stepped through the small door and the three of us followed, though it was hard for Kel to get through the small space, especially with Tisi in his arms.

As I suspected, on the other side, within the gate-tunnel, stood a small force of well-armed men in plate armor, with halberds at the ready.

"Please give the woman over to my men," the captain said. "Then we'll... talk."

Kel looked at me and Daz.

It was Daz who whispered: "Get her out of here, I'll make a way for you."

Kel blinked.

"Now!" Daz hissed and suddenly the guards and captain swayed in place, disoriented.

Kel pushed his way through them and sprinted into the city.

I couldn't join him, because whatever Daz had done had drained the last of his strength. He slumped on me, dead weight, nearly pulling me to the ground. And in the few seconds it took to figure out whether I should leave Daz and run or... whatever else... the guards had recovered.

I was trapped.

"What was that?" the captain hissed. "Phorasti magic?" He was furious, growling. "You'll pay for this, imposter!" And he stepped in to punch me. But I'd recovered from my indecision by that time.

"Sorry," I whispered.

The apology was two-fold, first to Daz, as I dropped him unceremoniously to the ground. Second, to the guard captain, who was simply doing his job, but I'd be damned if I'd let him stop us.

Using everything Tisi had taught me, I dodged the captain's fist and grabbed it as it passed my head. Then I pulled him toward me as I locked his arm and forced him down. I twisted his arm behind his back and hauled him up again in front of me, between me and the other guards.

"Let me through!" I hissed.

Only then did I realize I had a problem: I could use the captain as leverage and get past these guards, but I'd leave Daz behind. Or I could let the captain go and get Daz, but I'd lose my leverage. Which meant I was at an impasse. I was protected for the moment but couldn't go anywhere.

Well, fuck.

"Let me go, you fiend!" the captain growled.

"Tell your men to back off." That's when it hit me. "Tell them to go into the gatehouse."

The captain laughed. "Or what?"

I summoned every scrap of guile and moxie I could muster as I whispered in his ear. "You didn't think my friend was the only Phorasti, did you? How else could I look like your prince?" I might as well play into the man's suspicions and fears. "I don't want to kill these men, who are just doing their job, but I will. So, tell them to back off!"

In my hold, the captain went stiff.

"You wouldn't!"

"What's to stop me?"

"Back off, men! Get back into the gatehouse!" the man

shouted. The other guards hesitated. "Go! Now!" the captain yelled, and the men backed off, heading for the other side of the gate tunnel.

Now I just had to figure out what to do with this captain. I didn't really want to hurt him. There was one move Tisi had shown me, but it could be dangerous. If done wrong, I could kill this poor fellow, but I had few other options.

"Sorry about this," I whispered to the man, then brought my knee up swiftly between his legs from behind. I wasn't sure exactly what I hit, but the man gasped in pain.

Using this distraction, I released him then quickly reengaged with him, my arm around his neck. I had to make sure I pressed on the sides of his neck, not the front, that could kill him, which I didn't want.

I squeezed.

The captain struggled, but the kick to his nethers hadn't been so much to hurt him as to get him to exhale. The chokehold worked quicker this way and the man quickly went limp.

I was just a little proud of myself for using Tisi's training so well... even if I was ashamed that I'd had to use it on one of my own men.

The captain would regain himself soon, so I dropped him and picked up Daz.

I hauled the man — solidly built and heavy as he was — up onto my shoulder with a long grunt. Gods, I needed to get in better shape. I couldn't run with Daz like this, so I walked as fast as I could, staggering and stumbling.

I heard calls from behind me. Either the captain had awoken, or the other guards had come out again. I didn't stop to check.

I marched toward a side street, off the main avenue, as crossbow bolts flew past me. One grazed my shoulder and I let out a clenched-tooth gasp.

I made it around the corner, safe for a moment, but then, from the shadows of an alley, strong hands grabbed me and pulled me into the darkness.

"How'd you know I was here?" Kel hissed.

I hadn't... or had I? I could have headed in any direction, but... I'd felt a pull.

Curious.

"Let me have him," Kel said and took Daz from me. "Can you get Tisi? She's there." I didn't see him point, but again, I felt... a pull. I knelt as my eyes became accustomed to the darkness and found her form. I lifted her, finding renewed strength, and followed behind Kel as he moved deeper into the darkness of the alley.

"This way, not too far," he said as shouts echoed through the street behind us.

"Why didn't you keep going?" I asked.

"I would have, but I heard the captain's command for his men to back off and got curious. That was some amazing work you did back there. You've got some skill. Tisi trained you well."

Coming from him, that was no idle compliment.

"Turn here, almost there," he said, and we veered down another alley. We took several more turns in quick succession, then Kel stopped and set Daz down. We'd come to a three-way intersection of alleys. There was a door in the wall of the building where the fourth junction of the intersection would have been.

The calls of the city guard seemed to be all around us.

"If they didn't recognize me, they won't know to look here," he said as he fumbled with some keys. "If they did recognize me... well, then we're in for a very interesting night."

He shoved a key into the lock and turned it.

The door swung open and Kel whispered, "Babbling Brook!" Then he knelt and gathered up Daz, going inside. I followed, carrying Tisi, into darkness, hearing the door close behind us.

"What's going on, Captain," someone said, not Kel's voice. "It sounds like the city's in an uproar."

"A misunderstanding, but also... the city is under attack. The guards just don't know that yet. Take this man to my room. Leo, go with them, I'll be there shortly." This was Kel's voice. As my eyes adjusted, I saw the formless shadows of several other men around us...

This must be the headquarters of Drako's Dragoons! Once I realized that, I relaxed. Someone lit a lantern and light danced around us. Kel was already leaving the guardroom. Another man had Daz and nodded to me.

"This way," he said.

He led me to a large bedroom, which I assumed was Kel's.

I set Tisi down carefully on the bed as the other man did the same with Daz. He nodded to me and left.

Kel arrived — in full armor — a short while later.

He spoke as soon as he entered. "We have to assume Veora, looking like you, told the guards at the second ring gate to close up as well. We won't be able to get to the palace quickly or easily. But unless the city is in a full panic, they'll have to open the gates come morning."

"I don't know if we can wait that long," I hissed.

I had no clue what Veora was doing, but Tisi had been insistent we needed to get to the palace. I worried for my family. If Veora looked like me, she could go anywhere in the city... or in the palace. "Isn't there some other way to get into the city?"

Kel raised a single brow. "You're the prince. If either of us was going to know a secret way into the city, it would be you. Do you?"

"No."

"Then we have to wait for Daz to wake up, or wait for morning, or come up with another plan." He sat heavily in the chair behind the desk, his armor clattering.

He was right. Which meant, if I didn't want to wait for Dazar to wake, I needed to come up with some other way to get all of us into the city.

I paced.

Who would the guard let in?

No one. If the city was locked down the only people going in and out would be the guards themselves.

The guards...?

"Do you know anyone who could get us access to a few surcoats of the city guard?" I asked. I quickly followed up with, "And do you have armor that might fit me?"

Kel nodded. "I was just thinking the same thing, disguise ourselves as watchmen. It could work. When we worked for the crown, a few of my men had supple-

mented the city guard. I can get us access to the uniform."
He rose and came around his desk. "What about them?"
He motioned to Tisi and Daz.

"Hide them in a wagon?" I said with a shrug. "I was
only just starting on a plan."

Kel nodded. "Keep it up. I'll go get those surcoats and
some armor for you. Have you ever worn heavy armor
before?"

I shook my head. "No."

"Mostly we'll need to cover your head, but... yeah...
the rest..." He sighed. "I'll find something that works. Just
make sure you have a working plan by the time I get
back." He winked and left.

Great... leave me with the hard part.

What did I know?

First, I couldn't be me. Veora had done a good job of
making sure Prince Leonin wouldn't get in.

Second, the guards were looking for either me alone
or a group of four.

Third, they might recognize Kel just because he'd
worked for the crown, and few men in this city were as
large as him.

Fourth, whether or not Daz or Tisi woke up, neither
would be in any condition to help, at least in the short
term.

Fifth, if the second ring and inner ring gates were
closed, trying to get a wagon through would be difficult.
They'd be using the wicket gates only: to inspect
everyone who came by.

No... what we needed was a group of people, more
than just us four, who looked like city guards: just

another troop from the outer ring of the city. I hoped the gate-guards wouldn't suspect a group of six or more.

Which meant... we needed more than just a couple surcoats and a lot more men...

I ran off after Kel to let him know.

CHAPTER 4

KELRIC

I DIDN'T LIKE USING MY MEN LIKE THIS, BUT LEO'S IDEA WAS sound: a larger group wouldn't be suspicious. Twenty of my men had been helping the city guard and — luckily — hadn't yet returned their surcoats. So, we took sixteen men with us.

Leo wore chainmail and a surcoat, handling the armor like a champion... though I didn't know how long he'd last, with his wiry frame. Tisi and Daz were also in armor with surcoats. We'd roughed up the armor and uniforms, using some pigs' blood to make it look like they'd been in a fight. They were borne on stretchers, carried by two men each.

It was an hour before dawn. It had taken a bit of time to rouse the men, find the armor and equip everyone. A faint light in the east signaled the coming day.

Our troop marched up to the gate into the second

ring of the city. Since my voice or Leo's might be known, I had one of my lieutenants, a man named Chandres, leading us. He addressed the guards as we approached.

"Let us through, we have wounded for the infirmary." His tone was clear and possessed an air of command. There were a few healers of lesser note in the third ring of the city, but the official guard's infirmary was in the second ring, and with our "unconscious" friends, this seemed a reasonable way to go.

"What happened to you?" one of the gate guards asked after opening the wicket gate and calling back that we'd be coming through. He didn't question who we were.

Good.

"Is there fighting?" the guard asked, on edge.

As our troop began to file through the wicket gate, Chandres addressed the guard's concerns. We'd told him what to say.

"Those blasted Phorasti tore up the very cobbles from the street and threw them at us as a diversion. We lost track of them after that."

The gate guard paled. "Phorasti? I'd heard they'd attacked the outer gate, but I'd hoped those reports were false."

I had to duck low to get through the limited frame of the wicket gate.

On the other side, a man in a captain's uniform rushed up.

"There was another attack? Gods, you lot look horrible. What happened?"

Chandres stepped through the gate, the last of us. "I

need to get my men to the infirmary, then I can return and report," Chandres said, clipped but respectful. His fake rank was only a sergeant. That was the highest any of my men had been given within the guard.

"Yes, of course, return here directly once you're done," the captain said, waving us onward.

We'd made it.

We proceeded as if heading toward the infirmary but quickly slipped down a side street and out of view of the gate.

That... had been the *easy* part.

We'd not be able to use that ruse at the gate to the inner city. We'd have no reason to go through there with wounded. Luckily, Leo had a plan for that as well.

We slipped past the guard house and into an alley. Abandoning our guard's surcoats, we made our way down Outer Ring Road, around the second ring, to an expansive noble's estate. Leo was certain Veora wouldn't have come here, so he went in as himself. I went with him. The rest of my men guarded Tisi and Daz.

Leo's status got him passed the gates of the estate instantly and a runner was dispatched to the house.

Despite the early hour, three people — two men and a woman — came out from the large manor house as we approached.

The two men were both large and imposing... for noblemen. One was clearly older, silver in his dark hair and beard. From what Leo had told me, this would be Dagan Silvermoon, patriarch of the Silvermoon family.

The other man was clearly Dagan's son. Ferith Silvermoon was an almost identical copy of his father, just with no silver in his dark hair.

The woman was probably Dagan's daughter. Though given how nobles did things, she *might* be a young wife, but if so, she'd have to be a second wife, since the young man was clearly older than she was. She had heavy highlights of red in her blond hair, a strong strawberry hue, and her eyes were flashing forest green.

I recognized her as one of Tisi's lady students, from the time I'd observed a class. Leo had said her name was Lady Emarra Silvermoon.

It was clear all three of them had been up early, already dressed for the day.

"Your Highness," the older man said with a curt bow.

"Prince Leonin! What a surprise," Emarra quipped, stopping herself short of embracing him, perhaps because he was in armor, or maybe she sensed this wasn't a social call.

"What can we do for you?" Dagan asked.

"I have a strange request, but please know that it is of the utmost urgency. I do not have time to explain everything, so I hope you will trust that what I require is needed to save our kingdom."

That got their attention. All three looked a bit shocked.

"Whatever you need, you'll have it," Dagan said without hesitation.

"Good. Ready a carriage, a large one, and I will need Emarra to come with me when I leave and only her. Will that be a problem?"

It was clear Dagan had questions and concerns, but

he was addressing a royal. "No, Your Highness." He hesitated only a moment before adding. "But... I trust that an explanation will be forthcoming... eventually?"

Leo nodded. "Most assuredly. All will be explained in time."

Dagan looked from Leo to Emarra, then back. I understood that look. Leo was unmarried and so was his daughter. Perhaps there was some chance he could marry her off to a royal? The prince was showing interest in her, after all. But that wasn't going to happen. I hoped the large nobleman would understand, once he knew the truth.

Servants were called forth and sent to ready the carriage.

Since it was clear we'd have to wait, Dagan asked: "What *can* you tell us?"

Leo addressed the large man with a measured voice.

"A threat to the entire kingdom has entered the city and probably the palace. I need to get into the inner city, but without anyone knowing I'm there. This... threat... knows I'm aware of them and could have spies and informants everywhere. I need to get into the inner city undetected and get to the palace. Your daughter would not attract a lot of attention going into the city. I need to travel with her, hidden, and make my way to the palace to stop this threat."

All three of the nobles were stunned at this.

"A threat? Truly? And... informants, in our own city?" Ferith obviously didn't believe this tale.

"If the prince says it's true, it's true," Emarra said,

though her look suggested she was backing up Leo as a friend... but still didn't fully believe him.

"Will my daughter be in danger?" Dagan asked.

"No," Leo said quickly. "Once I'm at the palace, we'll send her away and she can return here safely. She need not escort me all the way to my destination to confront this threat. She is needed only to enter the inner city and palace compound."

Dagan nodded, clearly not happy but unwilling to further question a royal.

Perhaps to help the large nobleman feel better about this decision, Leo added, "The royal family will be grateful for your assistance in this. I cannot guarantee anything, but I'll speak to my sister, Queen Beatrice of Rolvan. Her son, Fredrin, is the heir apparent and roughly Emarra's age. I may be able to arrange something if the young man is not already betrothed."

Dagan's expression instantly turned to one of curious wonder. Emarra's turned dark. It was clear the father loved this idea and the daughter hated it. She said nothing.

The carriage arrived and Emarra, Leo, and I got inside.

"Gods' speed to you," Dagan said, then we were off.

"Do you really mean to pawn me off to your nephew?" Emarra was all hot indignation once we were away from her father and brother.

"No," Leo said firmly. "I said that only to assuage your father. I already know Prince Fredrin is betrothed. You're off the hook."

"Oh..." she said stiffly. "Well... good then."

Leo explained the plan to her as the carriage stopped where we'd left my men, outside the Silvermoon estate. There we quickly rearranged things. I would ride on the back of the carriage. An armored footman escorting the Lady wouldn't be out of place. Leo rode inside, no longer in armor, Tisi and Daz had been stripped of their armor as well and were carefully laid on the long side benches of the carriage. Leo would sit on the front bench, well away from Emarra, who would remain on the back bench. We'd keep the curtains of the carriage closed and only Emarra would address any guards who stopped us. She would tell them she was on her way to the palace. If the guards were adamant about no one going into the city, she was to insist, stating she had a royal writ of passage and if they stopped her, they'd have to deal with the queen. Leo had done his best job, mimicking his mother's signature and seal on a document he'd created earlier that morning.

As it turned out...the writ wasn't needed. We entered the inner city through the east gate, leading into the noble's district, well away from the turmoil we'd caused last night. The guards here were on edge, but less concerned about an attack. They seemed curious about a noblewoman going into the city so early but didn't stop her. Also... if there was trouble in the outer city, she'd be safer in the inner city as it was. The gates were opened, and the carriage rolled through.

We were in.

Now, we just had to get to the palace and find Veora...

Hopefully, by then Daz would be awake. Because without him... we'd have no hope of stopping the mystical madwoman. Yet by the time we'd reached our destination neither he nor Tisi were awake. So, instead of going into the palace, Emarra volunteered to take us to her family's "small" house nearby. They kept the mansion for times when her father might be called to long sessions of parliament and needed a place to stay in the city.

Emarra arranged things with the staff. We were shown to a sitting room where Daz and Tisi were laid on long couches. For the next part of our plan, we'd need servants' clothes, so Emarra requested some. She didn't ask why, but it was clear Leo would have a lot of explaining to do later.

Yet it seemed the limits of her restrained curiosity only went so far, when she asked, "What's wrong with Master Tisera?"

"She almost died last night," Leo said. "She was gravely wounded fighting an assassin who was sent to kill the queen. The man with her is her brother, a Phorasti who healed her, but was rendered unconscious by the effort." Leo's explanation was close enough to the truth to be believable. We didn't really know what Tisi had done, but there had been a dead man in the cellar when we'd all come around, so... it was a logical assumption that she'd fought him and won.

Lady Emarra seemed satisfied with this explanation and asked nothing more.

Now, Leo and I had a decision to make. We'd be hampered if we were constantly carrying around Tisi and Daz. So, either we waited for them to rouse or we went in on our own.

The two of us talked quietly as Lady Emarra kept an eye on our sleeping friends.

"To add to our woes," Leo said softly. "We have no clue what Veora may have done at the palace, looking like me. I might be in for a surprise when we get there... I'll have to be ready for anything."

I nodded and added: "What's worse, if she could be anyone, then even once we get to the palace, we can't just search for your duplicate. We'll have no clue who she is or where she is. Tisi is the only one who knows anything about what the woman was planning, which may not be much more than we know, but still..."

Leo growled in frustration.

I'd never heard the prince — usually so sedate and calm — make such a noise. It shocked me.

"We'll have to wait then, despite the time that might take. It means we may be too late to stop Veora, but if only the two of us go in... we'll just be stumbling around and probably not stop her anyway!"

"Perhaps I could go in?" I suggested. "Veora wouldn't impersonate me if she could be you. And it means if I find another prince Leo, I'll know it's her. My access will be limited, but I could at least do some reconnaissance."

"But how will we meet up later?" Leo asked. "And if the three of us do come after you, how will we know if you're the *real* you or Veora in disguise."

"We can use a code word." What was something Veora would never think of? "How about 'dancing ducks.' If any one of us is alone, we can use it to let others know we're us."

Leo nodded. "Sounds good. You go, I'll stay with Tisi

and Daz. Hopefully, if they wake up, they'll have a way to find you."

About that...

"When you escaped from the outer gate, you... you ran right to me. Did you...?" This was only a hunch, but... "Did you hear strange music before you woke up in the cellar?"

Leo's curious expression told me he had. "Yes. How did you know? Did you hear it too?"

"I heard something, yes. I... don't know what it was, but don't you find it strange that all three of us woke up together, all healed and well? Only Daz should have been able to heal us, but he woke up the same time we did. So... whatever happened to us—" this was the truly strange part, "—I think it was Tisi who did it, but I have no idea how."

Leo nodded slowly. "I agree. Though I also have no idea what happened or how Tisi might have done anything like that."

"I'm hoping it means Tisi will be able to find me if we're separated." It was just a guess, but I felt a truth to it.

Leo nodded. "Let's hope so."

I left soon after, heading to the palace. Leo's forged writ got me in. Once inside, I found a remote corner and changed into servant's garb.

I was in.

Now, I just needed to find a powerful, magical madwoman, who could be anyone.

Yeah... no problem.

CHAPTER 5

TISERA

I'D BEEN ALIVE, AWAKE. I'D FORCED MYSELF TO TELL MY guys about Veora... but then...

I'd returned to darkness.

There was no pain here. I didn't know if that meant I'd been healed or if I was closer to death.

And that strange music returned now and then. Right now, it sang an eerie and ethereal minor-key lullaby with the steady cadence of a march. I didn't know whether to succumb to slumber or rise and stride forward into this darkness.

The music seemed to be telling me something, but there were no words to guide me, only the feel of the sounds, the shape of the melody. My soul responded to the tune... but in no way I was familiar with. I'd never been one for soul searching. I was direct, a woman of action, of physicality, not spirituality.

And frankly, I was getting just a bit tired of this interminable darkness. So, I screamed at the music, bellowing into the void. My voice echoed back to me tenfold. So I roared back, this time gathering all that music to me, adding it to my howl of rage.

Light stabbed my eyes as they snapped open. I sat up with a jerk... still screaming. And within that split second after waking, before I fully came to myself, my scream echoed back to me. And with it came thousands of other unique melodies. Somehow, I knew... each of those songs was a life, a person in the city.

Then it all faded and I was just me, tired and weak.

"Tisi?" Leo came to me, sitting on the long couch behind me to help support me, which was good, as I almost fell back. I could still feel every one of my wounds from my fight with Dantoine. The flesh was closed over where they should have been, but I felt them, beneath the skin, still healing, still fragile and weak... like the rest of me.

"Fuck," I said, drawing out the word, relaxing back into Leo's arms. "I feel like I was trampled by a herd of horses."

"You... you were dead," Leo said softly.

"Fuck? Really?" Though... I could believe it.

"That's what Daz said. When we all woke up, you were torn to shreds. Daz said you were all but dead. He healed you but said you'd been so close to death that it was up to you whether your spirit returned or not. I've... we've been waiting for you."

"How long?" I asked. Had it been days or hours? Had Veora already succeeded in her plans?

"A few hours. It's early morning the day after... all that happened." He pulled me close into a gentle embrace and kissed the top of my head. "I'm so glad you're back with us."

"Here I am," I said with the flop of an arm: a weak and feeble flourish. I was trying to be brave and shrug off what had happened, but I was shaken by how close I'd come to death.

"Do you... feel up for a kiss?"

He had to ask? Did I look that bad? Though... I had been dead.

I nodded.

He was gentle, tender, careful as he tilted my head a little and pressed his lips to mine. I wanted more, I wanted hard and forceful and deep, but my body couldn't do any of that. I returned the kiss, weak and weary.

When Leo pulled back, still close, he whispered. "I... I thought I'd lost you. Seeing you there... the knives... and... so much blood, too much blood. Gods. I can't believe you survived that."

"It's what I do, the one thing I'm good at," I said with a weak smile. "I survive." I gazed intently at him when I added. "I love you Leo, I will always return to you."

"Yes, you will, won't you? I'll never doubt you again."

I looked around slowly. "Where are we?" I didn't recognize my surroundings. It was a sumptuous room, well attired and clearly speaking of wealth. But this didn't look or feel like any place I'd been in the palace.

"This is the Silvermoon manor in the inner city, Emarra helped us get here."

Oh... intriguing.

Daz lay on a couch nearby but... "Kel?"

"He's gone ahead to the palace to scout. You woke up long enough to tell us Veora was a threat, and to go to the palace, but we don't know anything more than that. Well, that's not true, we know she looked like me for a while coming into the city. That caused a lot of problems for us. And we're assuming she can look like anyone."

"Anyone she's kissed."

"Oh... I... you don't think...?" He flushed, clearly ashamed.

"I know she went to get you three, looking like me." I was still just a little angry that my guys had been so easily fooled by someone who obviously wasn't me, but then... I'd been fooled by Veora for weeks before that. I couldn't complain. "I'm assuming she kissed you then."

He nodded. "Yes, that's right." He grimaced. "Not my finest hour... in so many ways."

"No, it wasn't," I said, still just a bit peeved. "But now... you can make up for all of that." I smiled at him. "Kiss me again."

He did, deeper, if not harder and from that kiss I took strength. When he drew back, I thought... perhaps... I could sit up on my own.

I pushed away from him and brought myself upright, pulling my legs in to cross in front of me. Yet that bit of exertion left me dizzy and lightheaded. I swiveled to sit on the couch properly, the cushioned backrest very welcome.

"Fuck, I still feel so damned weak! I know I was dead and all, but... really?"

"Don't rush things."

I looked over at Daz. "Did he wear himself out healing me and the rest of you?"

"He healed you, yes, but he didn't heal us," Leo said.

That wasn't right. "Then who healed you?" I asked.

Leo shifted, pulling one leg up on the couch to face me. "Ah... well, Kel and I believe... you did."

I stared at him. "Me? How?"

He shrugged. "We don't know, but Daz woke up at the same time we did, and none of us were injured. I honestly don't... remember much after Veora... subdued us. I don't know if I was hurt much or not."

"You, no, but Daz and Kel were."

Leo shrugged. "Then someone other than Daz healed us. Daz was unconscious."

This was all just a little too weird. I said as much to Leo.

He grimaced. "It gets weirder. Before I woke up, I heard... music." He must have seen my reaction to that, my eyes going wide. "That means something to you?"

"Yes," I said slowly. "I... don't know what it means, but I've heard music too, before I woke up that first time and off and on since then. And when I woke just now... there was something... like a connection to everyone in the city."

I expected Leo to look astonished or curious or skeptical, but instead he just nodded, slowly, looking away. "A connection," he repeated.

"Does that mean something to you?" I asked, very curious.

His gaze returned to me intense but uncertain. "I... we encountered some trouble getting into the city. Kel and I were separated. Yet, afterward, I seemed to know exactly where he was. I ran straight to him. I shouldn't have known where he was, but... I found him easily. It was very odd and neither of us knows how it happened, but... I'm beginning to suspect something."

"Oh?" I asked, not entirely sure I wanted to hear this.

"Have you ever heard of Ikiosti?" Leo asked. "Did Daz ever tell you of them?"

The word was foreign to me. "No."

"They are Phorasti, like Daz, but instead of seeing auras as colors, they experience them as sounds and music. They use songs and sounds to influence people and affect the world."

"Fuck," I said as things clicked into place. "Veora! She's one, isn't she? She said she was a Phorasti, but different, and mentioned humming and singing to enchant your brother."

"My brother?" He blinked at that. "Oh, yes, Victor." He nodded. "That makes sense. Yes, Daz believes Veora is an Ikiosti."

My eyes went wide. "So the music I keep hearing is her?" No... that didn't make sense. If the music had healed Kel and Daz, then it wouldn't have been Veora.

"No, Tisi, the music is coming from you. I think *you're* Ikiosti as well."

Even as he said the words, I'd had the same thought.

But... no, that couldn't be the case. "I'm not Dathi," I said, confused.

"It seems the regular Phorasti — or Kromasti as they're known — are all Dathi, or at least the strong ones are. Yet anyone can be Ikiosti. Veora isn't Dathi." He shrugged. "I don't know much, and when I spoke to Daz about it, neither did he. Sorry, I wish I could tell you more."

I wished he could too. "So, I've got some mystical music power?"

He shrugged. "I don't know, but it seems possible. It fits the facts."

I sighed. "I... I'll figure that out later. For now, Veora is what's important. We need to stop her."

I filled Leo in on what I'd learned: Veora was Veronique — from Eromore — and had been using her powers to manipulate Prince Victor. She'd gotten him to push his wife and children away, even distance himself from his mother. Veora needed Victor to hate the queen for some reason. That was part of her plan. I assumed she'd make Victor do... something... but I didn't know what. I guessed it involved the queen but couldn't be entirely certain of that.

"Gods," Leo breathed. "I'd sensed a difference in Victor these past few months, but... I'd never suspected anything like this. I... I need to warn my brother."

I put a hand on his shoulder. "Leo, it's too late for Victor. He's lost to Veora's influence. But we should warn the queen and the rest of your family."

He nodded. "Yes, but... I can't just leave my brother to that witch!"

"We won't. I'm sure Daz will have some way to free him." Or so I hoped. I didn't know if Daz's color-magic and Veora's sound-magic could do the same sorts of things or not.

I looked over at Daz, still sleeping, peaceful and serene. "We'll need him before we do anything, though."

"Could... you wake him, with your powers?" Leo asked.

I didn't want to think about any of that now. "I have no clue."

Yet when I looked at Leo, his expression clearly said: *could you try?*

I sighed.

Standing would be my first challenge. I sidled to the side of the couch, then used the arm to help myself up. A wave of dizziness swept over me, but I managed to stay on my feet till it passed.

As long as I moved slowly, I didn't seem to overwhelm myself. Leo rose and helped me, holding me, as I shuffled over to the couch were Daz lay. I sat on the edge of the cushions next to him. Leo knelt on the floor next to me.

I felt weak as a kitten. I didn't see how I could wake Daz... or face Veora, in my current condition. But... who knew what I was capable of? I'd survived death, so...

I sat, looking at Daz, wondering what to do. Eventually my mind, still a bit sluggish, latched onto a possibility. I'd awoken by screaming into the void... but the music I'd been hearing was that strange lullaby march. Perhaps that song had been where I'd gotten the power to wake? Maybe it would work on Daz?

Now I just had to... sing it.

I grimaced.

I'd never been much of a singer. My father had said I had a beautiful voice when I'd been a child, singing melodies carelessly as children do. But I hadn't done that in ages.

I turned to Leo. "Don't laugh at me. I'm... new at this."

"I wouldn't dare," he said solemnly.

I nodded and returned my attention to Daz. There weren't any words to that haunting, rhythmic lullaby, so I hummed it, softly at first, then a bit louder once I was sure of the tune and cadence.

I put my hand to Daz's cheek, putting what force I could into the song and concentrating on him.

Nothing happened.

I didn't have time to waste on this, I needed to be strong and healthy and have all my guys behind me to face Veora. My emotions rose, swirling within me: hope and fear, determination and conviction.

And that's when I felt something. It shocked through me and into Daz.

He gasped and came awake.

The room spun as my light-headedness returned with a vengeance. Light dimmed. My vision narrowed.

I hoped someone would catch me as I fell into darkness once again.

CHAPTER 6

TISERA

LIKE SOME FAIRY-TALE, I WOKE WITH DAZ'S LIPS UPON mine, a soft and loving kiss. I lay propped in his arms as he sat on the couch.

"Thank the gods, you're alive and awake," he whispered. When he kissed me again, I felt *all* of his thankfulness.

I almost made a flippant comment about having to die to get a kiss like that, but... no. He kissed me like that every time.

When he drew back, I reached up to pull him down for another kiss... or I would have, if my arms had been working. Instead, I half-flung a semi-limp arm around and slapped him in the face.

As he stared at me in shock, I whispered, "I love you, too."

He laughed, probably mostly from relief and joy.

Then I laughed. Then Leo laughed, still on the floor next to us.

"And it's thanks to Tisi you're awake," Leo said to Daz.

I grimaced. I didn't want to talk about that now.

Daz raised a single brow then sighed out a long breath. "I saw colors before I woke, red and green, which are the colors of healing and revitalization. I thought..." He pressed his lips together. "There was an explosion of colors before I woke in the cellar too. But you can't be Phorasti, at least not Kromasti."

"She's Ikiosti," Leo said.

Daz nodded, lips still tight. It was clear he didn't like this. "As I'd feared."

"Feared?" I said softly. "Why? I healed you."

He sighed out heavily. "Just... to be sure..." He seemed hesitant. "You used some sort of song to heal me?"

I nodded.

"She sang it," Leo said, still seeming awed and curiously joyful about this, a counter to Daz's dour mood. "Well... hummed it actually. It sounded like some strange mix of a lullaby and a march."

"Blast," Daz swore softly.

"Daz? What is it?" I grew more and more concerned. Had I done something wrong? "What did I do? Is this bad?"

Only then did he look at me. He gazed at me for a long moment, then sighed and drew in a deep breath.

"No... it's not... bad." His voice was tight though. He wasn't lying, but he wasn't being entirely honest either.

"I just... it's not..." He sighed and shook his head. "That's a discussion for later. Right now, I'm very glad you were able to rouse me. Thank you for that." He forced a smile. "You still look rough. How do you feel?"

"It took a lot out of me. More than I was expecting. I feel even weaker now. I think some of my wounds have reopened."

He nodded. "Yeah, you have to watch that. It's very easy to give too much of yourself when healing. You can kill yourself if you're not careful." He smiled again, and this one seemed more genuine. "*That's* why I was so concerned."

I got the feeling he was concerned about more than just that.

He continued, "If I tried to heal you now, being weak myself, I'd just end up like you are. We need some food and a bit of rest."

"We can't rest," I said. "Veora has done something to Prince Victor. He's in danger. I suspect others in the palace are as well. We have to stop her!"

"I know," he said softly. "But... can you walk?"

"No, but—"

"Then listen to one who knows. I'll help you through this. There are meditations and exercises we can do to regain ourselves quicker, but we'll need lots of water and food and a bit of time. We can't get around that. If we're going to go up against her, we need to regain ourselves first."

He was right, as much as I didn't like it.

"Fine," I huffed. "Leo, can you grab us some food and water?" The prince nodded and left in a hurry. I turned to Daz and asked, "What do we do?"

"Can you sit up?"

I wasn't sure I should. I felt most comfortable lying down, not moving.

"I... don't think so. I'm pretty beat up and weak."

He nodded and carefully shifted, laying me so my head rested in his lap. "Then just stay still for now." He sat a little straighter and drew in a long breath. "Start by just concentrating on your breathing. You don't need to breathe too deeply if that hurts, just... notice your breath."

Yeah, with my wounded lung, big breaths did indeed hurt. So, I kept my breaths soft and full, without expanding my chest too much.

I focused on the air coming and going. This sort of quiet introspection wasn't natural to me, but the situation was dire. Daz and I needed to be well so we could face Veora... hopefully soon.

"Now," Daz said softly. "Try to imagine... ah... well, for me it's a color, green for life and health and the soothing peace of nature. From what Leo said a moment ago, I believe it would be a lullaby for you, soft and smooth and relaxing. I hope that's right." He grimaced.

I could see the tension in his features. Something about me being an Ikiosti grated on him. I would have asked what, but I suspected he wouldn't give me a straight answer.

That was an issue for another time.

"Try to... to hear it within your mind or even hum it softly," he whispered. "But... focus it inward on yourself."

While I'd been floating in that void, I'd heard a lot of lullabies, now I knew why. Perhaps I'd been healing myself without knowing it? I brought to mind a song Aunt Emri had sung to me when I'd been a babe.

Lay your head upon my breast
Time to close your eyes and rest
Let your cares all fall away
Through the night, by you, I'll stay
Slumber safe and slumber deep
I'll stay near to guard your sleep

Remembering that soothing melody brought a wave of nostalgia, making me feel safe and warm.

I had vague but happy memories of Emri singing to me, holding me in her arms, even once I'd been too big to cradle easily. She'd sit on my bed, and I'd lay in her arms or with my head on her lap — like I was with Daz now — and she'd sing me to sleep. I'd always felt so secure and loved in her arms.

So, I returned to the remembered warmth of Emri's arms, feeling tears of joy leak from my eyes as I hummed the tune and let myself sink into it.

And... I felt *something*... as if the warmth of my memories began to seep into my body. The aches and pains of re-awakened injuries began to fade, just a little.

"You may be able to feel your body repairing itself," Daz breathed the words. "If so, just let it do what it will."

We continued this for a bit, and when Daz instructed me to come up from my lullaby and regain myself, I opened my eyes to find Leo had laid out food and drink.

"Now drink and eat, just a bit, to restore your strength," Daz instructed.

Leo had brought several plates, some with meat, some

with fruit, some with heady cheeses. It seemed the Silver-moon larder was well stocked, which wasn't surprising.

Daz picked at some fruit and cheese, while Leo fed me and helped me drink. The food bolstered me, but I was still weak, unable to sit up on my own.

"That should be enough," Daz said. "Now... let's connect with our spirits. For me, that will be envisioning violet. For you..." He blew out a breath and shook his head. "I don't know what type of melody you'd need to regain your spirit."

He cursed softly, then drew another deep breath and let it out slowly.

"A hymn?" I whispered. I faintly recalled when I'd been about to die, slipping away, when I'd first heard music, it had started with a hymn.

"Why do you say that?" he asked.

I told him of my first experience with the music.

He cocked his head. "It... would make sense that your spirit would be what tried to keep you alive. It was all that remained of you when I healed you." He shrugged. "It's worth a try."

I didn't know many hymns, but I'd been to the temples enough on sacred days to remember a few.

Daz talked me through the next exercise, explaining what we were trying to do, how he could connect to his own spirit using colors.

It took some doing, testing out several hymns before a song connected with something deep within me. I sensed my own spirit, warm and bright and vibrant.

Then we spent some time focusing our power inward.

When we finished, I felt more alive and fulfilled, but still physically weak.

Then came another snack break, then another session.

This continued for some time, proceeding with various colors — for Daz — and songs for me.

Since Daz didn't know which song aligned to which colors, this involved some experimentation. Luckily Leo's extensive musical knowledge helped us match tunes to colors... eventually.

The color blue aligned with a madrigal, used to connect with the mind and confidence.

Orange matched with an aria, which connected us with our vitality, our internal fire.

We'd already figured out red was a march, connecting us to strength and love and passion. After that meditation, I felt strong enough to sit without assistance.

"Last, will be the most challenging, but will help you feel stronger," Daz said.

"There's more?" I sighed heavily.

He laughed at my surprised vexation.

"Yes. Bringing all the colors together into one, helps restore us as a whole. For me, it will be summoning white. For you...?"

We both looked at Leo.

"An anthem," he said with a shrug.

I knew he was right the instant he'd said it. That's what I'd heard just before I'd apparently healed all the guys, the rousing crescendo of an anthem.

I nodded. "You're right."

"Think you can summon one?" Daz asked.

I nodded as I snacked on some bits from the plates around me. After each session I'd been hungrier and hungrier, eating a bit more, surprised how much food I'd consumed.

"Then, relax, close your eyes and summon your anthem," Daz said.

I didn't know many anthems, only the rousing chorus for our nation's song, but not much more than that. Yet, even as I wondered if that would work, another song came to me, the song I'd heard in my spirit when I'd been dying.

It began soft, but with a strong beat, matching the pounding of my heart. It thrummed through me, slowly building. Then a spine-shivering key change brought soaring voices and rousing horns, bells, all supported by a thunderous unity of strings and pounding drums. It merged with me, shaking me to my very core and stirring my soul to vibrancy and action.

"Oh!" I breathed as it released me back to reality.

"What?" Leo asked. He was back with more food.

Daz still concentrated.

"I didn't hear anything from you that time. What happened?" Leo asked.

"I don't know if I can explain it," I breathed. "It was like nothing I've ever heard or felt before." I shook my head. "I don't know how, but I'm fairly certain I heard instruments I've never even seen before. Yet... I *know* this music. It's as much a part of me as my very soul and body." That song was *mine*, my power, my unique anthem.

I rose to my feet, testing my legs. I paced for a bit

before sitting again. I wasn't at full capacity yet, but I felt better than I had in a while. Also, I was famished. I dug into the food, finishing everything Leo had brought, so he went to get more.

When Daz emerged from his meditation, he asked, "Did you find it?"

"It's more like... it found me," I said softly.

He smiled. "Good." His smile then faded just a little as he sighed. "I'm... going to have to get used to you being an... an Ikiosti."

He looked up at me, eyes earnest. "There's nothing wrong with you or what you are, just my own training and prejudice. I'm going to have to learn to accept a new world."

"First, let's find Veora and deal with her." I touched his face, cupping his cheek in my hand. "Then we'll worry about the rest of this."

He nodded.

Kel rushed into the room. "Oh good, you're both awake. We need to move fast. Veora's wreaking havoc in the palace!"

CHAPTER 7

TISERA

"FUCK," LEO HISSED.

I agreed with that sentiment. Kel had filled us in on what he'd learned as we'd made our way to the palace.

Apparently the first thing Veora — as Leo — had done when she'd reached the palace was rampage through the servant's quarters, assaulting and kissing any female servant she found. The servants were now terrified of Leo, and the queen wanted to see her son immediately. The palace guards were searching for him. This also meant Veora could be any number of "invisible" servants in the palace.

We stopped in an alley not far from the palace.

"I can't go in there," Leo said. "If the guards find me, I'll have to answer for what Veora did.

"You can't go in there as yourself," Daz amended. "I

can weave a subtle illusion over your face to make you look like someone else, if you like."

"You're weak enough as it is. Can you afford to do that and still face Veora?" I asked. We needed Daz as close to full strength as possible.

Daz nodded. "Yes, it won't take much, illusions are simple manipulations of colors. Easy enough to maintain." He turned to Leo. "Are there Dathi servants in the palace?"

Leo nodded. "A few."

Daz stood before Leo, hands to either side of the man's head without touching. He concentrated, then Leo's facial features blurred and changed. Now he was a tall Dathi man with black hair and dark features.

"There." Daz sighed. He'd said it wouldn't take much out of him, but his shoulders slumped. He hadn't had that much to give. We'd restored ourselves to health and a little power, but neither of us would be able to do anything extreme for a while yet.

"What about Tisi and me?" Kel asked. "We'll be limited as to where we can go in the palace."

Leo chimed in. "It sounds like the guards will have other things on their mind. You'll be safe enough for now, as long as none of us draws too much attention to ourselves."

We all nodded to that.

We were dressed as commoners, servants, and Kel had learned the pass phrase for any new servants coming to the palace that day. We were soon inside the high walls.

It was clear the entire place was in an uproar.

Servants and guards alike rushed around on various tasks.

"So, what's the plan?" Leo asked.

Everyone looked at me.

I stopped to consider. "We know Veora's plan involves Prince Victor, but we don't know exactly what she's doing. I suspect we can't confront Victor. He may be hostile to us, and we don't want to hurt him. The best plan is to approach *other* members of the royal family and get them on our side first. I'd love to go after Veora directly, but she could be anyone and may be impossible to find." I considered only a moment before saying, "Princess Alice and my Aunt Emri would be the best place to start."

The others nodded and we made our way toward the royal wing. But we quickly encountered a problem. The main palace entry into the royal wing was closed off and guarded by a dozen men. There were several entrances through servants' tunnels as well, but the two we checked were also well guarded. Someone had put the palace guards on high alert.

In the end, we used a bit more of Daz's power to put four guards in one of the servants' tunnels to sleep. They'd be noticed quickly and when they woke, they'd know they'd been knocked out, but it couldn't be helped.

We passed quickly through the tunnels and out into the main halls. None of the servants' tunnels went directly into a royal suite. When we came around the corner toward Alice's suite, we saw another group of guards at her door.

We retreated back around the corner to consult.

Daz, the one who'd been at the palace the least, and

the one of us least likely to draw attention, was sent up to ask what was going on.

He returned with a grimace. "Apparently Prince Victor fears another attack and guards have been increased everywhere, but specifically around the royals."

And by Prince Victor, I was fairly certain that meant Veora.

"What do we do?" I asked the others. "We need to get past those guards."

Leo, still looking like a Dathi, chuckled. "Just one of us, a woman, might easily get past them. But... you'd need to have a reason." He quickly added, "It's early enough in the day, the bedroom attendant may not have come to tidy Alice's sleeping quarters."

I nodded. "You three wait here."

The guards eyed me as I approached, skeptical.

I think one of them nearly recognized me. The way he looked at me suggested my face was familiar. That wasn't surprising. I'd been at the palace a lot recently, and many guards had been there when I'd tested for the trainer position. Still, he said nothing. The man in charge decided he'd check in with Princess Alice to see if she knew me as one of her regular servants. I accepted this.

Emri came out, took one look at me, and told the guard that yes, I was safe and could be admitted. Once we were safely inside and away from the guards, she whispered to me, "What's going on?"

I didn't know how to answer that. So much had happened since I'd seen her last... and that hadn't even been two full days ago.

"Too much," I said. "I need to speak to Alice and the

other royals, things are happening that they need to know about." My tone must have been imperative. I could see she had more questions, but she just nodded and led me to Alice.

The frail princess rose when she saw me and took a few steps toward me, arms out to embrace me, but she stopped. "Tisi? What is it? What's wrong?"

"Everything," I said. "Please, Princess, sit. This is going to take a while to explain, and time is precious."

She nodded, sitting. Emri sat close to her, arm around her, like a protective mother.

I told them everything, blunt and harsh, I didn't have time for pleasantries.

"I need your help to get in to see Henry. If we can convince him, we can go to the queen, then hopefully we can save Victor."

"My Blessed Gods!" Alice breathed. "Yes, of course I'll help. I'll come with you to see Henry." She rose but faltered. Emri quickly stood to support the princess, keeping her from falling back to the couch.

"Tisi, Alice is weak. She can't—"

"She can if we help her. And she only needs to make it to the hall. One of my guys can carry her easily." I should have been able to carry her, but I was still not at full strength and didn't want to test myself and drop her.

"Tisi!" My aunt's tone was reprimanding.

"No, Emri, she's right," Alice said softly. "Please, I need to do this."

Emri looked from Alice to me, then nodded. The two of us helped Alice to the entrance to her suite...

"I'm sorry, Princess," the lead guard said as we tried to

leave. "I'm under strict orders from Prince Victor not to let you leave your—"

"Then you will have to decide, sergeant!" Alice's tone was stronger than I'd ever heard it, commanding and sure. "Whether you want to be dismissed by my brother or by me. If you do not allow me to leave, then great calamity will befall our nation and *you* will be to blame. You will never work for the royal house again!"

The man's eyes grew wide in shock.

"So, sergeant, what will it be? Will you obey me now, or obey an order my brother gave without knowing all the information?"

"Princess...?" The man hesitated. "I'm sorry." He bowed his head. "We shall escort you wherever you wish to go."

"That's better," Alice said, then all the fire went out of her and she slumped into Emri's and my arms on either side of her.

"Please," I said softly. "I have some others who can help, they are trustworthy." Then, without waiting for the guards to accept that, I shouted. "Kel, Daz, Leo, we need you!"

The three came running, and a still disguised Leo came to Alice and easily plucked her up into his arms. "I've got her," he said softly.

"Please take us to Prince Henry's suite," I said to the guard sergeant, and he nodded.

It wasn't far to the quarters of the fifth in line for the throne. A similar contingent of guards stood at his doors as well.

Alice had grown faint and wouldn't be able to

command these men, so I was a bit unsure how to approach them. Luckily, I was saved the trouble.

"Princess Alice must speak to Prince Henry at once!" the guard sergeant with us demanded of his counterpart. The other man hesitated briefly before he complied.

Our troop was admitted into Henry's suite... only to find — as we rushed into the main room — Henry being held by his wife, Princess Miraline, a knife to his throat.

It only took me a heartbeat to realize that wasn't Princess Miraline. The princess lay sprawled on the floor, blood at her temple, unconscious, hopefully not dead. That meant the one holding Prince Henry was... Veora!

We all stood stunned. Henry's two children, the young Prince Alfran and his sister, the tiny Princess Gwendolyn screamed and cried, standing off to one side of the room. It was clear there had been a struggle.

Even as I regained myself and charged at Veora, she turned Henry's head and kissed him. Then she tackled him behind a couch.

I ran around the large piece of furniture as Henry came up. "Kill the imposter!" he shouted, pointing at...

Another Henry who rose a bit more unsteadily. "No. I'm not... *He's* the imposter!"

I froze.

"Well... Fuck."

CHAPTER 8

LEONIN

"DROP THIS ILLUSION," I SAID TO DAZ AS I STRODE forward. Emri and Alice both gasped as I became myself again. I had an idea how to tell which of these two was the real prince Henry, but Tisi tried something before I got a chance.

"I killed Dantoine," Tisi said viciously.

Tisi and I searched for one of the Henrys to react, but Veora must have been stone cold, she didn't let anything slip.

"Who's Dantoine?" one of the Henrys said. The other just looked confused.

Now it was my turn. I moved up beside Tisi. "Only my true brother would know what he used to call me when we were children," I said looking at the two identical men before me.

"Cub!" one of the two shouted.

"That's the real Henry," I said.

Tisi leaped at the other one even as the fake Henry pulled a dagger out of nowhere and lunged at my brother. Henry was caught off guard and the dagger hit home, plunging deep into his stomach as Veora moved past him, fleeing into the prince's bedroom. She wouldn't be able to get out that way. There was only one way out of this suite and that was behind us.

Tisi followed close behind the woman.

I ran to my brother as he stood, staring, stunned at the wound in his gut. I caught him as his legs gave out and set him slowly on the floor.

"Daz, can you heal him?" I called.

"Yes, but..." I didn't know why he hesitated. He sighed and finished tending to Princess Miraline, then hurried over and began working on Henry.

Henry passed out, and I laid him back.

Daz quickly healed the wound, though blood still stained much of my brother's clothes and the floor around us. It had spilled out of him far too quickly.

Daz sat back heavily, putting a hand to his head, looking faint. "Ohhh," he sighed, then began to draw slow steadying breaths.

Tisi's Aunt Emri calmed the two young children, so the room was quiet when Tisi returned... swearing.

"Fuck!" Tisi bit out. "Well now I know how Dantoine got away last time. It seems Veora can make herself — or others, I'm guessing — fly. She just jumped out a window and circled around the palace. I couldn't follow her."

"We found her once, we can find her again," Kel said with confidence.

Yet Tisi countered quickly, "We got lucky. It was a fluke we found her here. She'll be far more cautious now that she knows we're all alive and hunting her."

That was true.

"So, we keep to our plan," I said with confidence. It would be a lot easier to convince Henry there was an assassin in the palace. And we needed him to explain things to the queen on our behalf, because I wasn't sure she'd believe the four of us, not after... *that* night.

But... Henry was out cold and I had no clue when he might wake.

"We can't wait for him to be well," Tisi said, growling the words.

"I'll do what I can to convince Mother," Alice said, her voice weak, but steady.

That would have to do.

"We should bring him with us," Kel said moving to me, indicating Henry. "We'll want the royal family all in one place, easier to protect."

"It would also be easier to kill them all at once," Daz said sounding a bit woozy.

We all looked at him. No one had wanted to hear that.

He shrugged. "What? It's true, and someone had to point it out. That might be exactly what Veora wants."

"Fuck!" Tisi shouted. "Why can't any of this be easy!" She stalked around, pacing for a time before calming a little.

"In that case..." She seemed to be coming up with a plan as she spoke. "Daz and Kel, you take Princess Alice, Emri, and their escort and head to the queen. She doesn't like either of you, but she's at least expecting to see Daz.

Leo and I will take Henry and his escort, find a palace physician, and hide him away somewhere safe. Then... we'll join you with the queen."

She grimaced. It was clear she didn't like the plan, but to me it seemed the best course of action for now.

"I agree," I said. "That sounds reasonable." It also meant I wouldn't have to explain to my mother about the assault on the palace servants. I wasn't looking forward to atoning for something Veora had done.

"You just don't want to face your mother yet," Kel grumbled.

True, but I wasn't going to admit it. "Can you think of a better plan?" I asked him.

He grumbled a negative, so we set about putting the plan in motion. Henry was a stocky and well-built man, I couldn't lift him, at least not alone. So, we got several of the guards outside to carry him.

I wished Daz and Kel luck and said good-bye — at least for now — to my sister. Then Tisi and I were off.

"There is no telling what Veora knows about the palace," I said softly. "You escorted her many times, what would she know from that?" I asked Tisi.

"A specific set of servants' tunnels, but I'll bet she knows more than that. If she could take Victor's form, she could have spent hours roaming the palace and no one would ever know. Wherever we put Henry has to be a place you're certain very few people know about..."

I smiled. I knew just the place.

"Then let's not keep him in the palace at all. This way!" I said, leading the guards down several halls.

"Where are we going?" Tisi asked.

"The temple of Aestric and Assa is attached to the palace so priests can come and go for special rites. The underground tunnel to the temple is known to most, but few ever use it and once there, I'm certain even fewer would know their way around. Also, I knew several priests who can help us."

"Good thinking," Tisi said with a grin. It was the first sign of hope I'd seen in her for a while. I was glad I'd been able to help.

We hurried through the palace to the temple, where I left Henry in the care of several priests I trusted. Henry's guards were left to guard the entrance to the temple.

Tisi and I hurried back to the royal wing, to face my mother...

We arrived in my mother's private audience chamber as Alice finished her account of things.

The queen focused her gaze on me and Tisi, a visceral disappointment and disapproval in those cold blue eyes.

After Alice had been silent a moment, Mother said, "If it had come from the lips of *anyone* else, I would not believe it." Her gaze swung back to Alice. "You and Henry are the only trustworthy children I have left."

Ouch.

The queen's gaze surveyed all of us.

"Alas, Alice, you are with a group which has proven untrustworthy, and I know you are a trusting sort. I don't know if I can believe you, given your story must come from these others. They were smart to have you deliver it, but all of this is just..." She huffed out a heavy breath.

"I never much liked Veora, and it is clear she turned Victor against me, that much is obvious, but the rest...?

Phorasti from Eromore... undermining us from within? Victor being *controlled* by the woman? It's all a little too much to believe... coming from the lips of those who have hidden so much from me already."

"I believe them, Mother," Alice said forcefully, which was saying something for the frail woman. "I may be overly trusting, but... have you been out in the palace today? Something is happening. I witnessed the attack on Henry." Alice turned to me, "Is he safe?"

I nodded.

"He's with the priests of Aestric and Assa in their temple, even I don't know where. I told them not to trust anyone, even myself, unless I was with another royal. I figured that should stop Veora from getting to him in any form," I said, staring directly at my mother. I then added. "Believe us or not, but we're going to protect you and our kingdom."

Mother returned my hard gaze, matching me stare for stare.

"Where did this mettle come from?" she asked, her gaze searching my soul.

I smiled slowly. "From Tisera. She gave me the strength to become who I wished to be."

"And who do you wish to be, Leo?" Mother asked with a note of disapproving curiosity.

My goal of being a general was no longer as certain, but that didn't stop me from knowing who I was.

"I am *not* a priest, and I am more than just a spare prince. I am a protector of this kingdom, a warrior, a poet, a scholar, and a lover."

"A warrior?" the queen said with a raised brow.

I gave a grimace, conceding the point. "I'm still in training, but I took on the entire west-gate guard, disabling their captain and knocking him out, and intimidating the rest to flee." That wasn't even an exaggeration either.

"You... did... what? When was this? Is that why I have half the outer city guard in an uproar?"

"Yes, sorry Mother. Veora looked like me when she entered the city and told the guards to apprehend anyone who looked like her... me. And they did their job well, but I managed to... ah... overwhelm them?" I wasn't sure if that was quite the right word.

The queen shook her head slowly. "Clearly there is far more going on here than I am aware of." She sighed and slumped a little.

Raising a hand to her forehead she massaged it, then ran that hand down her face. "Let's say I believe your story, what next?"

CHAPTER 9

TISERA

"WE NEED TO RESTORE SOME SENSE OF ORDER TO THE palace," I said, my tone firm.

I met the queen's gaze, though she intimidated the Hells out of me. "The trouble is, Veora could be anyone, telling the guards all manner of confusing and counter-productive things. We need to find a way to rein things in. At the same time, we should try to gather all the other members of the royal family. I doubt we'll find Victor easily if he's under her control, but hopefully we can still find his family. With Henry safely tucked away and his family here, they're the last ones. If we can start to return order to the palace, perhaps that alone with thwart Veora's plans."

The queen's gaze was shrewd. "You don't truly believe that."

"No, I don't. I think..." I hesitated.

"Say it woman. If what you say is true, time is short!"

"We need to find and *apprehend* Prince Victor. He is the key to all of this." My best guess was: "If he manages to kill you, then he'll be king and if he gets his family out of the way, Veora can be his queen."

The queen nodded slowly.

"I'd come to the same conclusion. It seems a likely plot. We just have no clue how or when or where. But you're right, restoring order to the palace and the city is our first step. Also, no one goes anywhere alone. We can't risk Veora tricking any of us again."

That jab was clearly at me and the guys. We had been tricked quite severely. She addressed the eight guardsmen, standing at the edges of the room. "You all shall be my messengers. Go out into the palace in groups of two. And for gods' sake stay together. Tell any other guardsman you meet that any orders they have been given up to now are void and that your orders come from the lips of the queen herself. If they are alone, they are to join with you until a pair of them can leave. If they are in a group, tell them they are to return here and hear the orders from my lips themselves."

Leo cut in. "Mother, what if Veora has managed to worm her way into a group of guards. That could bring her right to you!"

The queen hesitated. Then she turned to Daz. "Can you sense this woman? I thought you Phorasti could detect one another?"

Daz sighed. "We can... if we are being open, but we can also hide our auras from others. She can definitely do so, since she's fooled me before. I won't be able to spot her, but if I'm here, I should be able to counter anything she tries to do."

The queen nodded. "Then you and Captain Kelric will stay here with me to guard myself and the other members of the royal family." She turned back to the guards. "Your orders are to remain vigilant and bring order to the palace, calm the servants and nobles, while at the same time warning them of a hostile presence. Tell them to leave if they can. That will help. Let's thin out who our mystery woman could be. Now go, do as I have instructed."

The guardsmen saluted and departed.

The queen turned to me. "You and my son shall seek out Veora or Prince Victor or his family. If you encounter his family and you can verify they are all who they claim to be, then escort them here for protection. If you encounter Victor, subdue him and bring him here, guarded. If you encounter Veora... kill that bitch." I'd never heard the queen use that language before. It spoke to her level of fatigue and displeasure with this situation.

"We will, Your Majesty," I said with earnest intent.

She nodded to us. "Go!"

I left with Leo.

"That went better than I thought," he whispered once we were outside the private hall.

I had to agree. "Yeah."

"Where to?" he asked.

I shrugged. "Might as well start with Victor's rooms, I don't think we'll find anyone, but perhaps we'll find some clue as to where they might be."

He nodded and we made our way quickly to Victor's suite.

As we turned the last corner down the hall toward the suite, a guard, standing outside the door, saw us and ducked inside quickly.

I stopped.

"Did you see that?" Leo asked. "I don't know why, but I don't like the looks of it."

"That's because you have good instincts," I said. "The only reason for a guard to be so cagey seeing us, was if he was warned about one or both of us and—"

"The only one who would have done that is Veora," Leo finished with a brisk nod.

"Or Victor, depending on how in league with her he is, but yes." I sighed. "We're going to have a fight on our hands."

And here I was, once again, dressed as a peasant with no armor and no weapons other than a dagger.

"A fight made all the more difficult by the fact that these are palace guards. They're not doing anything wrong, just following orders. We can't kill them," Leo said somberly.

Right.

Fuck.

"That *does* make things more challenging." If we couldn't kill them or severely wound them, then they'd keep coming back unless knocked out, and knocking someone out quickly — while trying to fight others at the same time — was almost impossible.

I sighed. "Are you sure you're up for this?" I asked. He'd told the queen he'd taken on the gate guards and their captain. I didn't know how much of that was truth and how much was bluster.

Leo smiled. "You've trained me well. I can do this."

Gods, I hoped so. I didn't want to lose one of my guys and didn't want the kingdom to lose a prince. I nodded to him.

"Let's do this."

We each drew a dagger, our only weapons.

Drawing near, I noticed the door had been left slightly ajar. I motioned for Leo to keep back, against the wall. I too pressed my back to the wall, then reached out an arm to slowly push the door open wider.

A crossbow bolt sped through the opening. A shout followed, "That was a warning shot. We have no desire to hurt the prince. But if he sends in the witch, we'd be more than happy to deal with her."

Witch? I mouthed the word to Leo. "Do they mean me?" I whispered.

He grimaced, nodding. "My guess is Veora's convinced them *you're* what *she* is. In their eyes, you're probably the villain here." He pressed his lips together in thought. "But they don't seem to want to hurt me, perhaps I could go in and—"

"No, they might be bluffing and I'm not risking you. You're too valuable to me... and the kingdom."

"They're watching the door, so... what do we do?"

I wracked my brain, then smiled as an idea came to me. If they thought I was a villain and Leo wasn't, we could play into that. I quickly whispered my idea to Leo.

He grinned, nodding, then spoke, loud enough for

those in the room to hear. "What do they mean about you being a witch?"

"Nothing, Leo, you can trust me," I said back, voice raised.

"No, wait, what are you doing!" He did a good job of sounding alarmed.

I ran my dagger along the wall as we made various grunts and sounds which hopefully sounded like a fight. Then for the topper, I rammed the heel of my hand into my nose. It's not easy to hit yourself full strength, and I didn't, but it was enough. It stunned me for a moment, as blood ran down to my lip.

Leo looked stunned as well, I hadn't told him I was going to do that.

"Now!" I whispered then turned my back. He put an arm around me, "restraining" me, putting his dagger close to my throat. Then he edged me into view of the door. "I've got her!" he called out. "I'm coming in!"

My original idea had been for me to be the one behind, restraining him, but I just couldn't risk that they might shoot him to get to me. This way, if they did shoot me, Leo might have a chance to run.

The advantage to this ruse was both Leo and I could get a good look at the disposition in the room as we entered.

I didn't like what I saw.

There had only been four guards on Henry's and Alice's rooms. Four we could have easily taken. But this looked to be a whole squad of twelve guards, perhaps more in the other rooms of the suite.

Well, fuck.

They were spread around the room, well away from the door. Two were directly in front of the door and had crossbows trained on me and Leo. A small contingent of four men guarded the entry to Victor's bedroom. The other six were spread around the room, swords out, faces hard. I didn't know what Victor or Veora had told them, but it was clear they didn't like me much.

"Hand her over to us and we'll take care of her," one of the men said, viciously.

"Are you the sergeant?" Leo asked.

The man nodded.

"Good," Leo said and immediately released me and pushed me toward the man. I faked a stumble and dove forward, tackling the man mid-thigh, easily taking him down.

Someone shouted, "she's ensorcelled him," amidst other cries of alarm.

I smiled at that. Perhaps I had, but only with love. And now Leo and the guards *both* had to worry about fighting the other without hurting them... too badly.

I quickly pinned the sergeant, his arms under my legs. I put my dagger to his throat, knowing every second now was precious. "Tell your men to surrender!"

"Never," he spat at me.

It had been worth a try.

I clocked him with my other hand, a hammer-fist blow to his temple, sharp and quick. The first one only stunned him, the second one caused his eyes to roll up and he went limp, hopefully unconscious and not dead.

I threw myself off him and rolled to one side, coming up with my back to a wall. Five men headed for me, swords out in front of them. Leo was fist-fighting the two who'd had crossbows out. Smart man taking them out of the fight. The four guarding the bedroom door hadn't moved.

Five on one... with no armor, no surprise and only a dagger against their swords: I didn't like those odds. I'd do better in close, so I charged them.

They hadn't expected that.

I headed for the one farthest to the right, batting his sword out of the way with my dagger. Then, I threw the dagger at a second man, who flinched and backed off. At the same time, I put the first guard into a wrist lock and got him to drop his sword into my now free hand. Then I elbowed him in the neck to stun him and followed up with the pommel of the sword into his sternum. That one went down, gasping.

I set myself into a ready stance. At least I had a sword now.

"I don't want to hurt any of you," I said between heavy breaths. "That woman, Veora, she's the witch. She's bewitched Prince Victor. We need to save him!"

They hesitated.

Interesting. Perhaps they were uncertain about Veora or about how their prince had been acting recently. I pushed my advantage.

"You know I'm right. Think about the last few days, how has the prince been acting? I haven't been here, so it couldn't have been me."

Two of the four men I faced nodded to themselves, but the other two shook their heads and attacked.

I parried their strikes, backing off a bit to get clear of the man at my feet before he recovered.

"I don't want to hurt you," I repeated. "But I will if I have to, to save the prince. Don't force my hand!"

They did, pressing their attacks.

Well, fuck.

"You asked for it." I ducked a high slash from one guard, then rushed that one. I hit him hard with the force of my charge. He fell back with a huff of breath, while I'd remained on my feet.

I blocked a slash from the other man, bound his sword and with a flick of my wrist, sent it flying. I cut his sword arm hard enough to slice through the chain mail armor he wore. Then I kicked him hard in the gut, sending him to the floor.

Without slowing down, I turned back to the first, who was rising, and with a hard swing, I knocked the sword from his hand, then stabbed down into one of his mostly unprotected thighs. I aimed for the fleshy part, hopefully doing little real damage, but making it hard for him to walk.

"Enough of this!" I shouted, wild, my frustration and anger overflowing.

Everyone stopped what they were doing.

Leo had taken one man down, frozen in combat with the other.

Music rose within me — the even cadence of a march and the soaring voices of a raised hymn — as I said: "Drop your weapons and surrender!"

To my shock and surprise... they did.

CHAPTER 10

TISERA

EVEN LEO DROPPED HIS DAGGER.

The others let fall their weapons and raised their hands.

Whoa... that was...

I didn't have time to think about it.

"Leo, round them up, put them in there!" I pointed to the doorway across the suite from the prince's bedroom, probably a secondary bedroom.

Leo snapped out of his daze and began gathering up the men.

I went to the main bedroom. The four guards at that door had also surrendered, seeming stunned and confused. I moved past them easily. Keeping to the wall beside the door, I pushed it open. No crossbow bolts came through.

I peeked inside and grimaced.

There was Veora, with the prince's family lined up before her. The eyes of Princess Kira and her three children were glazed over as they stood perfectly still: enchanted.

"They'll protect me," Veora said, mostly hidden behind Victor's wife. "They'll happily throw themselves on your sword if you get too close."

"Whatever," I said, and tossed the sword aside. "How about now?"

The one eye I could see of Veora's — as she peeked out from behind her captive — went a bit wide. She hadn't expected that.

"I've seen you fight, Veora, or should I call you Veronique? You have skill. Why don't you come out and fight me, one on one, no tricks, just skill. Don't you want to know if you can beat me?"

She smirked.

"I won't fall for that. I may be skilled, perhaps better than any average warrior, but I will not underestimate you, Tisi. I don't know how you escaped from Dantoine, but if you're able to do that, then I certainly won't risk myself against you."

"Not even to avenge Dantoine? He's dead. He died... very painfully." This was a risk. I wanted to bait her, get her out from behind her wall of royals, but she might also get upset and send those innocents after me instead. "I still have all my lovers, but you've lost yours."

Rage filled her eyes, but she was too controlled to fall for my tricks.

Instead, she did as I'd feared and sent a royal after me. Prince Wilhelm was only eight years old, but he came at me like a feral cat, all nails and teeth and hissing fury.

I caught him and held him at arm's length, but I couldn't do that forever, with his small hands tearing at my arms.

I hummed a soft lullaby, just for him, and slowly he flagged and waned in his attacks, then his eyes drooped and shut. I set him down carefully to one side.

"H-how...?" Veora stammered. I could hear the fear in her voice. Her eyes narrowed. "You're Ikiosti. I can see it now, but why... why couldn't I see it before?"

I had a theory about that. "Dantoine did a very good job on me before I freed myself. I died or came as close as a person can and still return. And that's when these... strange powers found me." I laughed. "So... in a way... it's your fault I have them."

She smiled slowly. "Ah... so you're still new to them? Then you should be easy to deal with. There is no way you can match my strength!"

And she began to sing.

It was a complex tune, the cadence of a march, the soothing tones of a lullaby, the rising vocals of a hymn mixed with the complex lyrical pattern of a madrigal.

My body relaxed, my mind going just a bit unfocused.

Yet, even as this happened, some deeper part of me knew what she was doing. She was trying to put me to sleep, using all manner of complex threads to do so. All that was really needed was the lullaby, like I'd used with the young prince, but Veora did so much more. The Hymn connected to my spirit. The madrigal eased my wariness of her. The march added strength and dominance to the meta-physical attack on my senses.

I swayed. If I'd still been holding the sword, I would have dropped it, as my body weakened, going slack.

But there was no way I'd let her win that easily.

Some part of my mind instinctively knew the song I needed to counter Veora's attack and I began to hum it softly. It was a complex mix of march, aria, and hymn, with a slight mix of the other styles to create a soft anthem to clear away her influence. My mind cleared, my body strengthened, and I came to myself with a long breath.

"You... countered that?" Veora whispered in awe.

"It wasn't that hard," I said. It was the truth. I seemed to instinctually know how these powers worked. It was... natural.

"But..." Her eyes grew large. "No... you can't be..." Her face contorted in rage. "So be it!" she hissed and an instant later she put a dagger to Princess Kira's throat. "You can't get to me before I kill her." Her eyes lit with a venomous, savage fury. "Take one step and this bitch dies... right in front of her kids." She grabbed Princess Kira's hair and pulled the woman's head back sharply, exposing her throat.

I was curious why she was resorting to physical violence after only one failed attempt to bewitch me.

The answer hit me like a charging bull: she was too weak to try again. And in the next instant, I knew why... She'd been using her powers all day: disguising herself as other people, flying out the window of Henry's suite, swaying people to her commands. And she had three people she was trying to keep control over right now. For all her bluster... she had probably extended herself too far. Daz could tire easily if he used too much of his power too quickly. It must be the same for her. Whereas I, though still new to my powers and not at full strength, had done little more than run around the palace all morning.

Veora began inching away, toward a window. She hauled the insensate Princess Kira with her. The two children shuffled along, still in her thrall.

I couldn't let her escape. If she got to that window she could fly away once more.

So, I began a new song. Without knowing what to sing exactly, some part of me knew my intent and built on that. I wanted to gain control over Veora's body like she'd done with the three before her. I wanted to get that dagger away from Kira's throat and somehow do it secretly. So, the song was done as a whisper, barely heard, that would keep my effects hopefully hidden until it was too late.

The dagger moved, only an inch, but enough that it wasn't as much of a threat.

"What...? What are you doing?" Veora shrieked.

She resisted. Her arm quivered as we fought for control over it. Then slowly her hand opened and she dropped the dagger.

The two of us glared at each other as she realized she'd lost.

Veora dropped Kira and turned toward the window.

I charged in and tackled her before she got there. We crashed to the floor, rolling, and she ended up on top of me. Veora clawed at my face with long nails, consumed with rage.

I caught one of her hands, as the other raked over my cheek. I grabbed the other arm a moment later.

She screamed a ragged march at me, a bombardment of her powers, meant to overwhelm me, but I screamed back a more confident anthem... assuring my dominance.

Her scream escalated several octaves, losing its power, merely voicing her fury. Then, she drove her knee into my gut.

I released her as I coughed and gasped.

She jumped up, heading for the window.

I wouldn't let her get away. As much as these powers were coming instinctually to me, I didn't want to risk that I might not be able to fly on my first attempt. Which meant I couldn't go after her, I had to stop her, here and now.

I scrambled across the floor, snatching up her dagger and threw it. It hit her just below her right shoulder blade and sank in deep. She stumbled as she reached the window, gasping when she tried to sing.

I rose, breathing hard, stalking toward her. She attempted to reach for the dagger, but it was at an awkward place in her back, not easy to grab. When I got to her, I kicked her legs out from under her.

I hoped she'd fall sideways, but she fell back, landing on the dagger, pushing it deeper. The point of the dagger poked through her chest. Her eyes went wide as she twitched and writhed on the floor.

Fuck.

I needed her alive!

I knelt and tried to grab her, but she'd become a wounded feral beast. She thrashed about wildly, eyes half-glazed with pain and madness.

I slapped her hard, managing to stun her, then quickly rolled her onto her front and drew out the dagger. Blood frothed from the wound as she cried out and went still. She'd be dead very soon unless...

...unless I could heal her.

I didn't want to spend my energy on her, but we needed her alive, needed to know the full extent of her plan and what she'd done to Prince Victor. So, as much as I hated the idea, I sang a song of peace and soothing as I placed my hands over the fountain of blood.

The song gave me an awareness of the damage within her, and it was horrid. All that writhing had moved the blade around a lot. The dagger had shredded her lung and nicked her heart. I poured my song into her and tried to use her own strength and physical resources to heal the wound. The last thing I needed was to pass out... while she fully recovered.

I managed to repair the damage to the internal organs and stopped there, leaving a shallow wound in her back.

I swooned then, dizzy, the room spinning around me. I'd used too much strength, but Veora was alive... and also wouldn't wake any time soon.

I fell beside her, lying on my back, looking up at the ceiling, doing everything I could to remain conscious.

"Tisi?" Leo's voice. I lay on the other side of the bed. He couldn't see me. He sounded worried.

"Here!" I called, though it came out as a weak croak.

I heard his running footfalls, then he came into view. "Tisi? Gods."

"Make sure, she doesn't... escape!" I forced the words out as clearly as I could, flopping an arm to point at Veora. "I'm... just gonna... take a... nap."

I let my eyes close, leaving everything in Leo's care.

His arms encircled me as I fell into slumber. I wasn't dying, just exhausted, but I'd probably give him one Hells of a scare.

And... I'd captured Veora!

We'd won!

Well... sort of...

CHAPTER 11

Dazar

I'd been terrified when Leo had carried Tisi into the queen's audience chamber. Yet her aura had told me she was just unconscious.

And... somehow, she'd captured Veora!

Tisi rested now.

Veora had been revived so we could question her. But we'd taken every precaution.

First, we'd taken her away from the royals.

Second, Kel and I were the only ones in the room with her. A small contingent of guards were outside this room. They — and Kel — all had their ears bound with cloth, so as not to hear anything. Not all of an Ikiosti's powers needed to be heard by someone to be effective, but this should help. Kel also stood behind her. As long as he remained quiet, she might not know he was there.

Veora's wounds had been bandaged. No magical

healing used on her. I needed to be at full strength for this.

We'd tied her to a chair and would gag her once we were done, but for now, her mouth was free so she could answer our questions. That meant she could also use her powers, but I hoped she was too worn out from the morning's escapades. That was also why I was the one questioning her. Hopefully my Kromasti powers could counter anything she tried.

I opened my aura fully to her. I wanted to *feel* the instant her powers so much as flinched within her. So much as a flicker of color and I'd nod to Kel. He'd smack her, hopefully disorienting her, then gag her.

Allowing her to speak at all was a risk, but hopefully we were prepared.

Kel dumped a bucket of cold water over the woman, and she sputtered to life. Oddly, her first words were: "You healed me?" Her brow knitted. "Tisi healed me... didn't she?" She shook her head. "How did she get so strong so quickly?"

I wasn't about to answer any of her questions. She was here to answer ours.

"Enough, you'll answer our questions, or we'll cut out your tongue and hand you over to a torturer in the dungeons." I didn't know if Pearlia had any torturers, but I was fairly certain there were dungeons.

Veora recovered herself enough to glare at me, saying nothing more.

I took that as a good place to start. "What are your plans?"

"To make you my puppet, escape from this place, and

kill Tisi," Veora said with a nasty grin. Yet... none of her powers activated as far as I could see.

"What are your plans for Prince Victor?" I said, more specific this time.

"He'll do what I've commanded of him and either accomplish my goals or die trying." She smiled again.

"And what have you commanded of him?"

"Like I'd tell you any of that. Right now, I still have a chance for my plans to succeed. Kill me or maim me if you will, but if you do, I win. My part in this is over. Victor is your enemy now." She smirked. "Are you going to kill your own crown prince?"

She thought she'd won. Victor might be her pawn, but he hadn't acted yet, so far as we knew. We still had time.

We also hadn't found the crown prince yet, but everyone in the palace was looking for him.

"What do you mean your part is over?" I asked. Perhaps if it was over and done with, she'd tell us. Any information at this point would be useful.

A smile grew on her lips, I could see it. She wanted to gloat, wanted to tell us how cunning she'd been, how she'd already won.

I didn't say anything, just let her sit with those emotions until she shrugged.

"It won't hurt to tell you. You can't stop it. Even you, a high and mighty Kromasti could never undo what I've done to the prince."

She seemed to consider that. Then she laughed. "Well, perhaps you could, but it wouldn't be quick or easy and he'd fight you every step of the way. You certainly won't be able to undo what I've done in time to stop him."

"And what have you done?" I asked, again seeking specifics.

That arrogant grin spread on her face. "He is mine, completely: mind, body, and soul. My goals are his only objective. He loves me, that much was easy enough to accomplish, from there I just had to whisper a few things into his ear. It was surprisingly easy, actually. He already had some pent-up resentment for..." She caught herself. "Ah, but that might be saying too much."

Still, she grinned. "What I can tell you is that his entire life is dominated by my plans. He will not be easy to stop."

That was pretty much what I'd guessed. Complete domination. This was possible with Kromassa, but manipulating the colors of someone's aura was difficult. It took a lot of time and energy. Yet, Veora had had lots of time with Prince Victor. I didn't know if this sort of manipulation was easier for an Ikiosti, using words of power to speak directly to their thoughts and emotions, instead of manipulating the colors of a person's aura from the outside.

Perhaps.

I figured I'd try again to find out her plans. "If we can't stop your plans, then why not share them?"

She laughed. "Just because you can't stop them doesn't mean you can't put up a good fight. No, secrecy is my ally. And, as I said, my part in all this is done. I had only been manipulating the princess and Victor's family as... icing on the cake."

I didn't trust a word she said. I highly suspected we could still stop her plans and that manipulating Victor's family had been more than just a perk.

"I'll tell you this much, though," Veora said with that cat-like grin. "If you *kill* Prince Victor, that might... severely hinder my plans."

I took that with a grain of salt. It might be that killing Victor *was* her plan. No, whatever we did, we'd have to stop Victor while keeping him alive. He needed to remain safe, just... contained. I hoped we could manage that.

There was one other tactic I could try. "If you remove your influence on Victor, the queen might consider letting you go. End all this, and you might walk free."

Another laugh as she shook her head. "I can't remove my influence from Victor even if I wanted to. As you can probably see, I am not actively using any of my powers. I am not controlling Victor. It's always so hard actively controlling someone. It's far easier to subtly change their very nature over time. That's why you can't stop him with your magic because there is no magic to undo. What's done is done. I suppose you could try to undo what I did over the course of several months, but I *can* tell you... you don't have that sort of time. All you can do to stop him now is kill him."

She seemed very focused on us killing Victor, interesting.

I didn't think it would take as long as she was suggesting to remove her control over him, but still, it wouldn't be quick or easy.

"Then you've signed your own death warrant," I said softly, shaking my head. "All you can do now is mitigate that. Tell us what you know, and you can earn yourself a quick death."

"I'm tougher than I look. I've been trained to withstand torture and pain. I don't care if you kill me slowly. My family will be avenged!"

"Your family?" This was new information.

That superior smile of hers turned sour.

"Yes. My father and brothers died at Vestrea. My mother died of a broken heart from losing her husband and three sons. I am all that remains, and I vowed to bring down Pearlia if it was the last and only thing I ever did. And I've done that."

So, Veora — or Veronique — was indeed from Eromore. That hadn't been new information per se, but a confirmation of what we'd suspected.

That bitter tone of hers turned into a harsh and victorious laugh.

"And if you kill me, you kill Prince Victor as well. I've linked our souls. That was another fun bit of power I wove into my manipulations. If I die, his spirit will follow me into the afterlife. His body may be whole, but he'll be dead in every other way." Another laugh. "So, if you want to save him, you better keep me alive."

I didn't think that was possible with *any* sort of Phora power. She was either lying, to keep us from killing her, or she had some strange Ikiosti power unlike anything I'd ever heard of. It was at times like these that I cursed the White Tower for not educating us more on Ikiosti and what they could do. If I simply knew more...

I sighed.

"Is there anything else you wish to say?" I asked. It

was clear she wasn't going to give us any information we needed, and I didn't know what else to ask of her. I wasn't an interrogator.

She'd confirmed she was from Eromore, and her plan had been to influence Prince Victor. He was under her control, but not actively, the effect of months of manipulation. He'd not be easy to stop without killing him, which she kept mentioning. That made me believe his death might just be part of her plan.

She smiled, lips firmly closed.

I nodded, then I began a complex working of my Kromassa around her. She had — when she'd lured us to her house, after weakening me — spun a complex spell around me to keep me from using my powers. I would do the same to her now. It wasn't easy, like slowly plucking every hair off a person's body, threading my colors through hers to syphon them off, draining her of her aura and her power.

She felt it after a moment and her superior grin turned into a hard grimace. She knew what I was doing. It took me the better part of a half-hour, but I managed to secure her powers, at least for a day or two, a bit longer than she had on me.

I motioned to Kel that he could remove the cloth over his ears.

He did so.

"Take her away," I said.

He untied her and held her firmly as he escorted her to the dungeons.

I went to see the queen. Leo was there as well, speaking softly with his mother.

"Well?" the queen asked. "What did she tell you?"

I sighed. "Not much."

I sat heavily in one of the chairs around the long table before the queen's raised throne. "Mostly what we already know. Prince Victor has been completely and utterly bent to her will. There will be no undoing that without a lot of work and he'll probably fight us every step of the way. We still don't know what she has planned for him, but we can assume it had something to do with killing you and taking the throne, that is the only thing that makes sense to my mind."

The queen nodded. "To mine as well. Go on."

"That's pretty much it. She confirmed she's from Eromore, her family died in the last war. That could be a lie, but she seemed earnest about it. She also says that if we kill her, Victor will die. I don't believe it, but I wouldn't want to test it. I do not know of any powers that can do that, but that doesn't mean they don't exist. That's it. For now, I have taken her powers from her, she won't be a threat, at least not with Phora, for a day or two. Tisi says she's a better than average fighter as well, so she should not be underestimated in any regard. Sorry, Your Majesty."

The queen nodded slowly.

"I didn't truly expect her to give up her plans, but we did what we had to. We are not barbarians." The queen sighed. "Thank you, Master Stormhold... and... I'm sorry for what I'd asked of you before all of this."

She looked at Leo. "I've had a chance to speak to my son about your... odd... relationships with Tisera. I do not understand it, but I might eventually learn to accept it. I should not have acted so rashly when I found you all. Though... it was a bit of a shock."

I said nothing, nodding. I could understand how it might have been shocking.

Now we just had to find and save Victor before it was too late.

CHAPTER 12

Tisera

I woke to a gentle kiss upon my lips.

"Hello, my princess," Leo said softly leaning over me.

"Did I get her, did we capture Veora?" I asked groggily as I came awake.

Leo smiled. "Yes. She is secure now, do not worry."

I slowly sat up. I'd been placed on a large bed in a massive, well-appointed bedroom. But I'd seen all the royal bedrooms, and this wasn't like any of the others. Unless... the only bedroom I hadn't seen was... "Is this the queen's chambers?" I breathed.

Leo smiled. "Yes."

The thought of being on the queen's bed... with Leo... made me blush, which was truly rare for me. "Oh."

"Daz is resting. He may know of a way to find Prince Victor with magic, but he needs some time to regain his strength. Until then..." He shrugged.

Kel entered, carrying a large tray laden with warm meat, heady cheese, ripe fruit, and fresh bread.

My mouth started watering. Kel brought the tray to a large table in a sitting area by the windows of the room. I felt better, rested, but still weak. So, Leo helped me up and let me lean on him as I walked over. I sat on the plush couch next to Kel.

"I'm famished!" I said. Apparently, all this magic stuff made me hungry.

We ate in silence. Well, Leo and Kel ate in silence, watching me stuff my face. Though I wasn't speaking I wasn't exactly quiet either. Everything just tasted *so* good. I moaned and smacked my lips while my two guys smiled and shook their heads at me.

We were all a bit surprised when Daz entered.

He plodded over to us and sat down heavily next to Leo, across from me and Kel.

"Can't sleep. Too much on my mind. I don't really need to sleep, just rest. As long as I'm not exerting myself too much, I'll regain the power I need soon enough."

"Is it difficult? Finding a man using magic?" Kel asked.

Daz grimaced. "No, but that's not what I'm doing. If I was just finding him, that would be easy, but it seems Veora hid his aura from me."

"Oh?" Leo said softly. "*Can* you find him, then?"

Daz nodded. "Yes, but instead of looking for a man I'm now looking for a void where there should be an aura, which is a lot more difficult, hence why I need the energy and rest."

Curious.

"Is there anything we can do?" I asked, feeling refreshed and invigorated after my rest and a good meal.

"No," Daz said softly.

Kel chuckled. "Well..." he drew out the word. "There is *something* we can do." We all stared at him, not getting his vague reference.

Kel looked at me, then the bed... then me, then the bed, then Leo and Daz.

"No," Leo breathed. "My mother would kill us! We can't. Not in here."

"We can if we lock the door," Kel said mischievously.

And suddenly everyone was looking at me, their gazes intent, hot with kindling passion, but seeking permission. Apparently, I had the final say.

"We just... have to keep it quiet." I couldn't help the massive grin spreading on my face. "Kel, lock the door."

Kel laughed and rose to do as I'd asked.

"Fuck me," Leo moaned.

"I intend to," I quipped, loving his look of surprised arousal, a blush on his cheeks. I rose and went to him as he spoke again.

"If Mother finds out she'll..."

I straddled him and stopped his words with a kiss. Then I drew back and whispered, "Then let's not tell her, shall we?"

I kissed him again. This time he responded with hot passion and pressing need, arms encircling me to hold me close.

I rocked my core over him, feeling his cock harden more and more with every pass. There was too much clothing between us.

"Take me to that massive bed," I breathed.

He grinned. Though, there was still a look of trepidation in those glorious sea-green eyes. I could see how using his mother's bed might be awkward for him. "Unless you'd rather...stay here?" I asked, voice breathy, while grinding myself on his lap.

Leo sigh-laughed. "No." He looked at Kel, who laid the bolt in place securing the door. The large man nodded.

I slid off Leo as he rose. He scooped me up into his arms, carrying me to the bed.

"Have you gotten stronger?" I asked surprised by this.

"I had to carry him recently." He nodded his head toward Daz. "I'm feeling a bit stronger these days."

Leo laid me on the high, soft bed. Daz joined us, standing on Leo's left, then Kel arrived on Leo's right.

My men.

My gorgeous men.

All together and with such hunger in their eyes. How could a woman resist?

"Last time, I was in command, and that was... so very hot, but I want this time to be for all of us," I said.

"Something tells me, you'll still get the most out of it," Daz said with a grin.

"I'm good with that," Kel whispered.

"Me too," Leo added.

Daz looked around. "I'd hate for us to have to restrain ourselves... vocally that is, but..."

"What?" I asked.

He looked at me, expectant. "I could try to weave a

barrier of sound around this room, but your powers are more directly suited for it, since you work with sound."

I didn't want to think about my powers right now, I wanted these three men to ravish me. But I couldn't deny his point. If I was going to be ravished, I wanted to be able to scream my bliss.

"I can try. Any idea how?"

Daz smiled. "I have a vague idea, I can guide you through it. First, you'll need to do it all at a whisper, for that is the sound of secrets and hidden things. Then, I believe you'll need a song somewhere between a lullaby and a madrigal. If it were a color, it would be aqua, the color of peace and tranquility. Then you may need to add a bit of a march for strength to expand it out and set it in place."

That sounded complicated.

I closed my eyes and sought peace within me, sought the silence of my soul. Then I gathered my power, taking the silent serenity inside me and wishing it to be all around us.

As had happened before, instinctively I began to sing.

It baffled me as I listened to the tune I voiced. It was everything Daz had mentioned: the softness of a lullaby, with the metered lyrics of a madrigal and just a bit of a march's surety for strength.

Everything went completely silent. I couldn't even hear my own song, though I still sang it. Then a bubble of sound popped around me, and I could hear again.

Each of the guys experienced the same thing: lips moving, but silent. Then I saw their surprise at being able to hear again, as my bubble expanded. I pushed it out to the walls of the room, then sung a crescendo of power to set it in place. It drained me a little, but since I'd just rested and eaten, I felt well enough to go ahead with some mind-blowing sex.

"It's done," I whispered.

"Is there any way to test it?" Leo asked, just a bit apprehensive.

"Attack on the prince! Guards!" Kell bellowed. We all flinched, our ears ringing at the intensity of his powerful voice.

We waited.

No one came running.

Kel shrugged. "If no one came running for that, then they won't come for much else. We're good. He looked at me, you can scream to your hearts content."

And I would.

I knelt on the bed, gathering the hem of the peasant's dress, then lifting it off me, tossing it away.

Three sets of eyes — sea-green, caramel-gold, and dark-sable — devoured my naked form.

"What are you waiting for?" I asked, voice breathy.

Leo began to undress, moving with swift precision. Daz waved a hand and his clothes flew off him. I'd seen him do similar things before, commanding cloth. Kel didn't bother stripping. He climbed onto the bed, circling behind me.

"I can wait," he said, hot breath on my cheek as he knelt behind me. "But *you* need loving, now." Strong arms encircled me. The rough warmth of his hands on my skin sent a shiver through me. He swept them up to grasp my breasts, massaging with thick fingers.

I moaned, leaning back against him.

"Yes," I whispered.

Then his hands shifted to my sides, and pressed close, tracing down to my hips and out over my thighs before me. He ran those strong hands over my legs, down to my knees before shifting in just a little to help push my legs open, then both hands swept up to the apex of my thighs, pressing firm to either side of my folds.

"Touch me," I begged. I closed my eyes, head resting on the massive swell of his shoulder, focusing on his caresses.

He waited, kneading my thighs, building a wonderful anticipation before...

One thick finger slowly circled my folds, gathering my wetness, before pressing lightly on my clit. I shivered with a thrill of bliss, opening to him.

Feeling a kiss on my cheek, I turned my head to his, eyes still closed.

His lips came to mine, kissing softly, deeply, as his hands moved up, over my stomach, back to my breasts. I moaned into his mouth, wanting more attention at my core.

I gasped as another hand found my folds.

Breaking off with Kel, I looked to see Daz shifting closer on the bed. His lips met mine as his hand traced lines of bliss-fire over my opening, his power thrilling into me. I moaned loudly into his mouth as our kiss deepened.

"Lay her back." Leo's voice was soft but commanding.

We all shifted.

Kel moved out from behind me and helped me lay

back. I stretched out my legs as Kel and Daz reclined to either side of me. Leo knelt on the bed, between my legs but too far away. The tall tower of his erection throbbed, but he seemed oblivious to it, leaning down to kiss my stomach, then moving his lips lower.

Reflexively, I tilted my hips up to meet his mouth as he kissed my folds. His tongue slid over my slick heat, darting inside me, tasting my depths before he shifted and began sucking on my clit, tongue circling and flicking over it wonderfully.

Daz and Kel each found a breast with their lips. Daz kissed lightly, brushing his tongue over the swell, then sucking softly on my raised nipple. Kel was hard and needful, raking teeth and hard kisses. When he found my nipple, he clutched the nub carefully in his teeth and flicked his tongue wildly over my tip as he slowly drew his teeth along the standing flesh.

A boiling need consumed me, bubbling up from my core and sizzling out to my extremities. Waves of liquid heat washed over me as my guys drove me higher through a shivering escalation of bliss.

Kel left my breast and brought hard kisses to my lips. I circled a hand around behind his shaven head and pressed him closer, even as I slid the fingers of my other hand through Daz's thick short hair and pressed him harder to my breast.

I set my legs on Leo's shoulders, rocking my core against his mouth.

So close!

And when Leo's suction and flicking tongue hit me just right, I found a soft-shuddering climax. My twitching legs tightened around Leo's face as I gasped into Kel's mouth and my arching back pressed my breast harder into Daz's attentive lips.

I let go and succumbed to the pleasure, letting it lift me as my three amazing men pleasured me orally.

This was so very hot, so amazing. I hadn't realized how much I'd needed this.

And we were only just beginning.

CHAPTER 13

Leonin

Tisi's body went slack, loose, as the throes of her orgasm faded. Her legs relaxed, no longer pressing tightly to my cheeks. I eased off my insistent devouring of her glistening, heated folds, kissing her lightly and looking up to see what she wished for next.

Kel had released her lips, lying beside her, one thick-fingered hands still teasing the taut peak of a nipple. Daz traced lines over her stomach as he kissed her arm and shoulder on the other side.

Tisi wore an expression of beatific bliss, smile a bit sloppy. "Wow," she breathed between heavy gulps of air.

She looked at each of us in turn, her gaze locking on mine, full of love, desire, and appreciation.

"What next?" Kel asked.

"I want a moment with each of you," Tisi whispered. "First Leo, then Kel, then Daz. The others can... help, but

I want to enjoy each of your unique bodies... then I want to have you all together." She actually giggled, perhaps still elated from her first orgasm. "Is that too demanding?"

"If it is, none of us are going to complain," Kel said.

Daz and I made noises of agreement.

"Oh, good." She grinned. "I didn't know how much I needed this until I had it. Gods, but I love you all so much!"

"I love you too," I said softly, as Daz and Kel murmured similar things.

"How do you want me?" I asked, slowly caressing my hands over her thighs.

"On your back." She began to rise. Kel helped her up. "I'm going to ride you like the stallion you are."

Sounded good to me.

I lay back, taking Daz's place as we all shifted. Tisi straddled me, staying low over my legs at first. She reached down and ran her hand over my length: slowly, softly, caressing.

"Sometimes I forget how long you are," she said as she stroked me gently. I liked the soft playful touch.

I smiled up at her. Each of us men had our own unique attributes, and I was just a little pleased I was the longest of the three. That didn't really mean much — since the two others were both excellent lovers — but I still took pride in the fact.

She looked me in the eyes, gaze hot and intense, but also honest and heartfelt. "I love the way you feel inside me. You press so deep, and those orgasms are so intense!"

She lifted her hips over me and positioned me at

her opening. She teased her folds, moving my tip around her molten moisture. She even rubbed me vigorously over her clit, closing her eyes to enjoy the sensations. Then she moved me down and let my tip slip inside her. She played there as well, shifting her hips around in a slow circle, her wet heat pressed around me.

I slid my hands up her thighs to her hips, then up farther to her breasts, kneading them softly as she slowly lowered herself onto me. Her hands came to my chest, leaning forward as she took me deeper.

She gave a shivering breath when her folds finally pressed to my loins. My tip buried in her sacred depths. Her sultry canal gripped me so hard I felt the beat of her heart.

"Yes," she whispered as she began a slow rocking, which kept me pressed deep while stimulating her clit.

I slid my hands down, one slipping between us, to lay there, giving her a bit more to grind her clit against as she moved over me. The other hand I kept on her hip to feel that sexy rocking.

Daz and Kel moved to either side of her. She turned, from one to the other, kissing and being kissed and caressed. Eyes closed, she moved by feel, her glorious form swaying over me.

Her pace quickened.

That lithe, strong body trembled, shivering with delight.

My cock swelled as I watched her ecstasy mount. This was going to be a slow but powerful peak when she reached it, and I wanted to be ready to come with her. So,

I kept myself under control, at the pinnacle of pleasure, waiting for my final release.

She shook and whimpered, having trouble keeping herself upright. The other two held her, strong hands supporting her while caressing her flushed skin.

Then, finally, she pulled away from Daz's lips to gasp: "Oh, gods! Yes!"

She bucked, convulsing through a release. Her core clenched around my shaft as she shuddered, crying out in bliss.

By all the gods, she was sexy. I couldn't help myself, the sight of her enraptured made me lose control. I came, my cock pulsing hard inside her.

"Oh, gods!" Her voice rose an octave. "Leo! Oh! Yes!"

She pushed Daz and Kel away, hands rising to clutch at her own breasts as she leaned back just a bit, still moving over me with sharp, hard motions, extending her bliss. I slid my hands up to her sides, keeping her in place as she rode out the powerful pressure of her release and mine, joined together.

"I love you, Tisi. Everything I have, everything I do, is for you!" I proclaimed, pouring out my emotions.

And when she'd finished, she lowered herself to lay upon me, her body the perfect mix of soft and hard.

She kissed me, fiercely, our tongues driving deep, breathless. And when she rose just a little, pulling away, there were tears of joy in her eyes.

"Thank you, Leo, that was... everything. I love you."

"I love you," I repeated, and she smiled. We kissed again, an attempted devouring before she slowly pulled away.

"Now," she whispered. "Make sure you're ready for round two." Then she carefully rolled off me, onto her back, beside me.

I lay in heaven before Daz chuckled somewhere nearby. I blinked and found him kneeling next to me.

"Tisi *loves* to make a mess," he said.

I pushed myself up to see, a little horrified at the wet spot surrounding my hips. "Fuck," I whispered. "Mother's bed!"

"Don't worry," Daz said softly, with another chuckle. "I can clean that up. It'll be good as new after we're done." He looked over at Tisi, lying on her back, legs open and raised, holding her ankles as Kel moved up to her. "But something tells me this won't be the only mess she makes, so I'll wait."

I had a feeling he was right.

And I didn't regret anything. That had been one of the most blissful moments of my entire life.

And we weren't done yet.

CHAPTER 14

Kelric

Tisi looked up at me with a haze of bliss clouding her gaze.

"I want you to take me, just like this." She held her legs, spread open and pulled up, knees on her shoulders. Her hands on the back of her calves kept them in place. Her folds were open and raised up before me, slick with her and Leo's mingled releases.

"Fuck me hard, Kel. I want to feel your strength." She rolled her head to the side. "And you two, I want you close by, I want your cocks in my hand while—" She returned that fiery gaze to me. "—while Kel makes me come."

I'd stripped while Tisi had teased Leo, before they'd truly begun. I loved the way Tisi's amber eyes roamed my naked form, hungry and heated. Her lips were just a little parted, tip of her tongue between them. Gods, but she was so undeniably sexy.

Thinking of how she'd asked for it reminded me of all the times we'd been together during the war, hard and needful, pounding with pent-up fear and lust. Those times had been quick, stolen from the night. I would make sure what we shared now was anything but.

I knelt close, lowering myself until my cock was at the level of her thrust-up hips. Leaning on one arm, I held my cock with my other hand and teased my thickness over her swollen, sensitive, and slippery core.

"Oh," she hissed softly. "Yes!"

I was at an odd angle, since her hips were thrust upward, but I used my thumb to press the tip of my cock down into her opening, thrusting shallowly, as I played my fingers over the slick nub of her clit.

"Deeper," she whispered.

Daz and Leo had positioned themselves, one on either side of us. Tisi released her legs and reached out to them, grabbing their cocks. Daz gasped but kept his cool. Leo's needed a bit of working up again. I tried not to be too distracted by them, concentrating on my love.

Her legs relaxed a little, rising up until her ankles rested on my shoulders.

I levered myself up and forward just a bit, putting more weight on my one arm, which pressed deep into the soft bed. My other hand I kept between her legs, circling and flicking her clit as I began to thrust deeper. I did one slow plunge down into her hungry heat and watched her eyes roll back, lips pressed, body squirming.

"Hard," she whispered. "Make me scream."

"As you wish," I said and removed my other hand from her folds. I pressed it into the soft mattress so I could thrust with all my might down into her. I pulled my legs up close for leverage, then drove myself relentlessly into the molten mess of her pre-pleasured core.

My own need gripped me, flashing through me in a wave of super-heated desire. I roared as my body seemed to blaze forth with that heat and I plunged all the harder and deeper within her. The wet slapping of our bodies was barely audible over our combined cries.

Tisi was well worked up, already simmering with pleasure. I brought her back to a rolling boil, giving her everything, all of me.

We were both panting and crying out, no words, just raw expressions of exertion and pleasure. Then she went stiff and cried out all the harder. Her core grasped my cock, milking me, even as she flooded.

Peak number one.

I slowed my heavy thrusts, sitting back. I put my hands on the tops of her blazing-hot thighs, pressing them close to me. Then I crossed one leg over the other such that her feet were to either side of my neck on the opposite shoulder. This pressed her opening tighter around me. I leaned forward and grabbed her breasts, letting my full weight press on them as I gripped the soft flesh. Her nipples dug into my palms as she squirmed and gasped through the last of her orgasm, then began whispering semi-words, which sounded like pleas for more.

"As you wish, my love," I breathed.

I slid my hands down to grasp the front of her thighs

and began thrusting hard once more. Her release gave me all the lubrication I needed to move free and quick, driving myself into her.

She released the two cocks she'd been stroking. Her hands dug into the sheets, curling up balls of the cloth as her head tilted back, her body arching. She looked exquisite in the throes of passion: the glimmer of sweat on her body, the rapid rise and fall of her chest with each heaving breath, the way her body shook every time my body slammed into hers.

Gods, it was almost too much. Her rapture nearly made me come. My cock swelled, and suddenly she wasn't so loose around me anymore.

"More!" she cried out, and some power tingled through me, starting in my gut, then tickling down to my loins and...

"Fuck!" I grunted, pausing while buried deep inside her. What was this sensation? It felt like my cock had grown, larger than it should be: long and thick and powerful. Somehow, she'd given me a super-erection: heavy and awkward.

"More," she whispered again, and I figured I should give it to her before she made me even larger!

With a roar and a savage thrust I filled her again, then continued my rough pounding as Tisi writhed and twitched in the throes of purest passion.

She cried out, drawing her legs down off me, pulling them to her reflexively. Her sheath wrung my entire length and pulled it deeper, throbbing around me as she came... hard. Then, she erupted with so much force it pushed my cock right out of her.

She thrashed about, arms and legs pounding the bed as she screamed with such utter rapture, it was almost scary. I grabbed her flailing legs, stilling them with my strength before opening them to dive back into her. Instantly, her legs went around me, wrapping tight, pulling me closer. Eyes and mouth wide, she gasped around hard-shuddering breaths as her body continued to undulate wildly. She was trying to speak but couldn't. I took her meaning clear enough.

Grabbing her hips, I resumed my savage thrusting. Her back arched as she keened a high squeal. She reached up to rake her nails over my chest and abs, leaving angry red lines. Then she seemed to levitate off the bed, hands going around me to find my ass. She dug her nails in, squeezing my cheeks and pushing me deeper. She couldn't form words but the look in her eyes was clear, imploring. She needed my release.

I gave it to her.

Overcome with her feral sexuality, I erupted inside her.

Eyes clenched shut, head tilted back, she opened her mouth in a silent scream. Tears leaked down her face as she twitched, shivering and shuddering. Her core contracted around me milking me as I emptied myself, giving her everything I had.

It seemed to take forever before my cock finally flagged and her body stilled. I pulled her close to me in a fierce embrace, pressing my lips to hers as her eyes opened again.

"What was that?" she asked softly between nibbled kisses.

"Amazing." My only answer.

"No... your cock, it seemed to... grow..."

I laughed. "*You* did that."

"What?"

"I think it's this new power of yours. You whispered 'more' and suddenly there was... *more* of me."

"Oh," she breathed.

"Don't worry, I'm back to normal now," I said, uncertain if she was concerned about the change.

"Oh." She sounded vaguely disappointed.

I laughed, which caused all manner of interesting reactions and aftershocks of bliss. Once we'd recovered from that, I whispered to her, "Anytime you need... *more* from me, all you have to do is ask. I love you, Tisi."

"I love you too, Kel." She smiled tenderly.

We separated slowly, and she lay back, dazed in bliss before her smile widened. "Time for round three," she whispered.

She was insatiable.

And I wouldn't have it any other way.

CHAPTER 15

DAZAR

MY COCK ACHED WITH NEED FROM WATCHING MY BELOVED experience so much ecstatic pleasure. More than once, especially when she'd been squeezing me as Kel had ravaged her, I'd nearly come. I'd had to use a hint of my power to keep my cock from exploding.

But now it was finally my turn.

Best for last.

"How do you want me?" I asked as I leaned over her, kissing her softly.

She grinned up at me, reaching up to push me away as she rolled over. She tucked her legs under her and thrust her ass up. Turning her head to the side, so it wasn't pushed into the sheets, she looked back at me. "I want you like this. But first, can you use a little of your power to make me tight again?"

She was indeed loose and wet. I didn't have to, but I

reached out a finger, slowly running it around her opening as I used red, sienna, and orange, with a little bit of healing green to reinforce her tired and lax muscles.

She gasped at the faint thrill I'd instilled in her as well.

"It won't take much," she gasped. "I'm soooo ready. Just... take me, hard and I'll come for you."

That sounded good to me.

Still, I wanted to give her a bit more than a few perfunctory thrusts before we came. So, I slid my hands over her back, using just a hint of power, healing green and red for strength. I massaged the colors into her back muscles and listened to her long, soothing sigh of bliss. That would give her a reserve of strength and energy to play with so we could truly enjoy this moment together. I slid my hands back to her buttocks and around to her hips as I drew close. My raging erection found her now-rejuvenated opening, and I played, slipping my head around the well-lubricated area.

She hummed her pleasure at this. Then I pressed my large tip against her opening and with a very slow push of pressure inched myself into her. This was the most precious part for both of us, the feel of my large head entering her. And once my tip was fully inside her, we both let out a moan of gratification.

I pushed deeper, until I was fully inside her, then paused. I slid my hands down her sides and lifted her, slowly, until she was heavy against me, back to my chest, leaning on me.

"Don't you want things... quick?" Her words were

slightly slurred, eyes glazed with ecstasy, head resting on my shoulder.

I shook my head as I raised my hands to cup her breasts. She shivered with the contact.

"I want both of us to enjoy this," I whispered, then kissed her, though the angle was awkward. As I did, I brought my forefingers and thumbs together, gently pinching her nipples.

She moaned and squirmed. "Much more of that and I won't last long," she whimpered.

"What about this?" I asked as I slid a hand down to her clit and slowly flicked three fingers over it. One. By. One.

I got a gasping intake of breath for each brush, then a ragged breath. "Gods! Daz... fuck me, please!"

How could I resist that?

All my life I'd wanted to be more than her adopted brother. I'd yearned to be near her, with her. And here she was, begging me to fuck her. We'd come a long way in a short time, and I was over the moon with the intimacy of our relationship now.

I began thrusting, softly, slowly, even though we were both more than ready. I kept one hand on her clit, maintaining a firm pressure there, while the other held her tight to me, occasionally seeking a breast to grasp and knead.

I didn't need any power at all to sense her overwhelming aura of sienna and red. It was intoxicating and... so much more powerful now that she'd discovered her abilities. I'd thought her aura to be stunningly strong *before*, but now... it could easily inundate me. So, I gave myself over to its power and simply added my sienna to hers.

"Yes," she breathed, voice hoarse. "Yes, more, just a little... oh!" She shuddered and squirmed as her sienna exploded around me, her body's orgasm a miniscule thing in comparison with the release of bliss within her aura.

And with that bloom of power, her colors mingled with mine, a force within my spirit. Her need was a whirling tornado in my soul, pulling me into its torrential power, helpless.

My body reacted, thrusting, needful, vicious. And her body and aura reacted to that as we continued this frenzied cycle. Tisi's pleasure spiraled upward, growing more and more powerful. Her body trembled in waves of bliss, which blasted through both of us, until I could resist no longer. My power was nothing in the face of her need. She whipped away any restraint I had.

My release came as a surprise. I kept thrusting before I realized I was coming, and then I drove myself deep and let myself go. It was, unequivocally the most powerful and mind-blowing orgasm I'd ever had.

Tisi's sienna exploded as she came again, finding the pinnacle of the storm of passion we'd built up. The tempest of her desire drenched us body and soul as it ever-so-slowly dissipated, making both of us lose our minds to its unrelenting power.

I came to myself a bit later. The two of us had collapsed together, now with her atop me on my back. We were a sweaty mess of limbs and gasping breaths.

Leo and Kel knelt nearby.

"And you wanted more after this?" Leo asked, a bit agog.

Tisi answered between gasping breaths. "I... may have... misjudged... how..." she left off there.

"Amazing?" I prompted.

"Yes... Amazing... you all... are." Then she let out an uncharacteristic giggle. "But I still want... all of you... inside me... at once."

She rose on trembling limbs and slowly extricated herself from me. Then she flopped down next to me, captured my face and brought it to hers in a long, deep kiss.

"Thank you for that," she whispered, words just for me. "It was amazing, you're amazing. I love you."

"You're more than amazing," I whispered. "You're celestial, transcendent!" I had to let her know how powerful that had been for me. "I love you too."

One last kiss, deep and sure, then she pulled away. "Can you be ready again... now?"

It would take more power than I wanted to spend right now when I should have been resting, but I would... for her.

I'd do anything she asked. "Yes."

"Then let's have one more hurrah," she said, then giggled, then shivered with expectant bliss.

CHAPTER 16

Tisera

I was tired and weak, covered in sweat and tears. My pussy was a royal mess of mingled releases, loose and sloppy, but buzzing with remembered bliss. I'd be so-very-sore tomorrow but didn't care right now.

We all had to shift to find a dry spot on the queen's bed. Daz mumbled something about taking care of that, for which I was thankful. The queen had apologized to us, and I didn't want to upset her again. Though some spiteful part of me thought this a fitting punishment for what she had done to push us away from each other.

"What do you need?" Leo asked me.

"All of you," I said, voice slurred and sloppy, like me. "Figure it out."

I was floating on a cloud of bliss and just wanted one more ultimate prize before resting for a while.

Strong hands moved me. I was laid on my front for a

while as Kel's thick fingers, slick with oil, massaged my rear entrance. Daz would be too tired to do his usual thing. Also... we hadn't brought any oil... which meant the queen had a stash of oil in her room. I applauded her for having a healthy sex life.

Leo massaged my back, though I was already limber and loose, not a single tight muscle in my entire body. Kel tested my rear opening: first with one finger, then two, then three. Finally, he entered me, giving shallow thrusts.

We were ready to begin.

Kel lay on his back. I was maneuvered on top of him and once again, carefully he pushed into my rear entrance. I sat on him, feeling his throbbing cock deep inside me: so deep, so full! Gods!

I was laid back carefully. Kel's strong arms slid down and scooped up my legs as Leo straddled Kel and drew in close to me. Gods, Kel already felt so very deep inside me, and Leo would be... I shivered with anticipation as Leo slid easily into my folds, pushing himself deep.

Kel released my legs, and I wrapped them around Leo, pulling him in tight, feeling that amazing length of his buried inside me.

Then came Daz. I reached out and waved him to me. He shuffled on his knees until my hand could cup his sack. I massaged it as Leo and Kel began moving inside me, then I lost all rational thought and action and simply grabbed Daz's cock, bringing it to my lips. He hadn't fully revived yet, but a few hard strokes of my hand while I played my tongue over his large tip, and he was at full strength once again.

Since I'd already had too many orgasms to count, this

was mostly a reward to my guys for the amazing experiences of earlier. I wanted them to have more... of me, and my love.

But that wasn't to say I wasn't getting anything out of this. Despite my sloppy, loose and lazy body, Leo and Kel's alternating strokes were quickly stoking my passion from embers back to a blazing bonfire. And the way Daz used his fingers to burn lines of bliss on my breasts was making them ache with arousal. Daz's fingers spiraled around one sensitive swell, up and in until he traced a tight circle around the nipple, his power pulsing into me. That would have been enough, but then he softly flicked the nub of my nipple and I moaned with my mouth around his cock. By the time he'd done the same with the other side, I was an inferno.

We were all a bit tired, all aroused beyond reason. And I knew exactly how to bring this moment to a perfect end.

I slipped Daz's amazing cock out of my mouth and gave my warning. "Be ready, I'm going to... ah..." I looked up at Daz. "What was it called when you gave me pure pleasure?"

He smiled, the hand that wasn't tracing lines on my chest combing through my hair. He shrugged. "It doesn't really have a name."

"Oh." It didn't really matter. "Just... be ready," I warned everyone. Then I wrapped my lips around Daz again and sought the music inside me.

I knew the intent, the effect I wanted. I'd experienced it before. Daz would say it was sienna, but for me it was a powerful aria-march, which matched the rapid beat of my heart. I delved into it, let it enfold me with its power. And since this could be dangerous, I tied a condition into the melody: play for only a stanza, then fade.

Then... I unleashed it on myself and my lovers.

Pure.

Powerful.

Mind-blowing.

Bliss.

Raw sex and desire roared through all four of us. Joining me in an extended, perfect orgasm, were three other bursts of utmost ecstasy. We were all brought to the brink, where the extremity of joy met the razor's edge of pain and even the risk of death.

Then the song ended, and we all collapsed into a heap of heart-pounding, exalted rapture.

Gods!

My heart raced, pounding so hard I wasn't sure it would ever calm.

Leo, Kel, and Daz all gasped for air. I could feel their heartbeats — pounding as hard as mine — through their throbbing erections. Curious, I reached up to lightly cup Daz's sack. He gasped with a shiver of pained-bliss at my touch. His balls were high and tight, twitching and contracting, over and over, giving me all of their precious gift.

Leo collapsed on top of me, placing soft kisses over my chest and shoulders. Daz trembled as he finished. I worked his cock with my hand, making sure I had every last drop of his release before he withdrew and half-collapsed on top of Leo.

"Gods," Daz whispered. A sentiment echoed by the other two once they could speak.

As for me... I was complete.

The heat of sex faded into a warmth which enfolded me, a soft and comforting blanket of love, desire, devotion, and unity which strengthened my spirit and resolve.

Eventually, we all extracted ourselves and cuddled together. Daz lay on one side of me, close and resting. On the other side lay Leo, with Kel behind him, holding us both.

"We've utterly ruined my mother's bed," Leo said softly, then oddly laughed at that, sounding just a little manic.

"I'll fix it... later," Daz mumbled, dozing. He needed his rest.

Kel chuckled. "Serves her right. She didn't want us doing it in your bed so..."

That made Leo laugh all the harder. I joined him.

When that died down, I spoke with earnest devotion. "I love you all." I sighed. "I don't know how this strange family of ours happened, but I know I couldn't live without any one of you."

"Neither could we," Kel said. I hadn't expected such a quick agreement from him. "I know now, it has to be... all of us. I alone could never love you as *we* can." He rubbed Leo's arm affectionately. "We're a team now, a family, like you said. Sorry princeling, but either your mother gives us all titles or you'll have to give up yours. I don't think we can be together as we were meant to be otherwise."

"I'd gladly give up my title to be with all of you," Leo said. "We are one entity now. Kel and Daz, I see you as extensions of myself. We are three-hearts-made-one with love for this perfect woman." He kissed my shoulder.

"Far from perfect," I said with a laugh.

"Perfect for us," Kel amended.

"That... I can agree to." I sighed, feeling so very seen and loved and happy.

Kel drew in a long breath. "And..." he drew out the word. "Our perfect little team should probably join the hunt for Prince Victor. At least Leo and I can, you and Daz might need more rest." He leaned over Leo and kissed my forehead. "Ready, princeling?"

"Are you going to keep calling me princeling?" Leo asked as the two of them began to move away.

"Is that a problem, princeling?" Kel chuckled to himself.

Leo cringed, then laughed. "I give up."

"Good choice, princeling." They slid off the bed and headed for their clothes.

I curled up closer to Daz and gave myself over to rest.

When I woke, the sun had shifted considerably, falling in the west. Leo and Kel were gone, and Daz was up and dressed. He looked up as I rose and stretched, his gaze taking all of me in.

"Rest well?" he asked, smiling.

I nodded then rose, sliding off the bed, which had been cleaned. I ran my hands over the fluffy sheets.

"Did you...?"

"I didn't feel like being exiled by the queen, so yeah."

I stretched again, mostly just to watch Daz watching me. It still amazed me that I had — not one, but *three* — men in my life that looked at me that way. And to think that only a few weeks ago, I'd thought myself unworthy of love. Back then, Daz had been my adopted brother. Now, I couldn't imagine him as anything other than a lover. Leo hadn't even come into my life yet, but now he was a fixture. I'd hated Kel, now I couldn't see my life without him.

I found my dress and slipped it on. "What are you doing?" I asked, interrupting him. Other than ogling me, he seemed to have been concentrating on something. He sat on a couch, legs folded in front of him, hands palms-up on his knees.

"I was searching for Prince Victor, a void within the storm of souls and auras."

"Oh... then I won't interrupt again."

He laughed. "No worries, I could actually use a bit of a break. I've already searched several parts of the palace, but to no avail."

I sat on the divan across from Daz and sighed.

"Since you're resting... can we... talk?"

He sighed and nodded slowly. "I thought this might be coming." He gave a second, heavier sigh. "I'm sorry, Tisi, there really isn't that much I know about your powers."

I pursed my lips. He'd hit on exactly what I'd wanted to talk about.

My powers.

"Still, can *I* talk?" I asked. I was a bit concerned and confused and hoped that maybe talking about it might help.

"Of course," he said with a nod. "What is it?"

He seemed at peace now, accepting of what I'd

become... what I was. I was so very thankful for that. He'd been so disturbed and appalled when he'd first learned of my powers. I was glad he'd come around.

"I... I..." Gods, these were the hardest words to say. "I'm afraid."

CHAPTER 17

Tisera

There, I'd said it.

I'd faced death and battle, sieges and horrors of war, and I had come through all of that. I hadn't thought there was much left in this world that could terrify me.

It wasn't having these powers that scared me, so much as... "I... I can do things so easily, almost without trying. I'm terrified of what I might do... by accident."

Daz raised a brow. "Oh?"

I explained. "I don't know if you noticed or heard us talking about it after, but... when I was having sex with Kel, I... well, he was thrusting so hard and it felt *so* good, but after Leo, I just wanted a bit more from him. I wanted him deeper and bigger and... are you okay with me talking about this?"

Daz smiled and gave a soft laugh. "I've come to terms

with the fact that being with you is going to be interesting and complicated. I... I always want you to be able to come to me and talk to me about anything, even sex with Kel, so yes."

"Good, thank you, Daz. You're being so wonderful about this." I gave him my most sincere smile and continued. "Anyway, I wanted more from Kel and my intent was so pure that when I voiced the words and asked for more... I *affected* him. I made his cock bigger."

"Oh? I *did* miss that." Daz's tone was a bit shocked and also curious.

I sensed an unasked question and answered it now, just to get it out of the way. "And no, I'm not going to make your cock bigger."

He laughed, blushing a little.

Men.

I sighed.

"Daz, don't you see. I did that without even *trying*. I affected another person without even consciously knowing it. Admittedly, it was in a good way... *this time*."

I left unsaid the obvious: *what about next time?*

And... there was more. "Then, when I brought all of us to pure bliss, I did that without humming or singing anything!" It was my turn to blush. "My mouth was... otherwise occupied."

Daz's blush deepened, since he'd been the one *occupying* it.

"Anyway, that time again, I just... had a strong intent and I heard the music within me and... it happened."

Daz nodded slowly, his mood shifting to serious. "And

you're worried you'll do that, in a bad way, to someone, by accident."

I nodded.

"It sounds like you tapped into a rather substantial reserve of power when your Ikiosti abilities bloomed within you. Now... you need to learn control."

"Yes, control. Any thoughts on how I do that?"

Daz sighed deeply. "For Kromasti, it's a long road. Our powers can easily overwhelm us."

He grimaced and looked away. His voice was soft when he said, "Just being near people with strong auras can stun us, knock us out."

He looked at me intently. "You, by the way, have an *incredibly* strong aura, perhaps stronger than anyone I've ever known, even the Phorasti Masters at the White Tower. You were potent in spirit even before your powers bloomed, and now you're..." He smiled softly, comforting. "Don't worry too much, but I do have to actively work to keep your aura from overpowering me."

"Oh? Truly?" Wow.

"So, yeah, if you were able to learn a bit of control that would help... both of us." He rose and came to sit next to me, arm around me, holding me close.

"At the White Tower we were given meditations, ways to control our mind and spirit and powers. I... I don't know if they'll work for you, but we can try."

"Yes, please. What do I need to do?"

He removed his arm from around me and we shifted, each facing each other on the divan, my hands in his. His caramel-gold eyes were intent.

"It took me the better part of a year to learn this, but I'm sure you'll get it in an instant. You've always been like that, so... amazing." He smiled. "Now, try to calm your mind. Clear it of all thoughts. For me... I focus on black, the absence of color, the void. For you... perhaps try focusing on silence, or a whisper, the hidden sounds."

I did as he instructed. I closed my eyes and tried to block out all but the sound of Daz's voice.

"I find black the hardest color to work with, since it isn't a color at all. White is hard, because it's all colors, but that just requires more power. Whereas to summon black one must push away all colors, which is antithesis to a lot of what a Kromasti does. Perhaps that's why it took me so long to learn this. But if you can find the silence..."

Daz's voice began to fade, growing quieter as I closed off from all sounds.

There was a familiarity to this place. I'd been here before. My heart lurched when I remembered when and why: I'd been here when I'd been dying. This was the void, the absence of all senses.

I started at that revelation and sounds came rushing back as I fled that memory.

"Tisi? Tisi? Are you... you were—"

My eyes snapped open, and I reached over to Daz, quickly pulling him to me in an awkward and trembling embrace.

"Tisi? What happened? I... I couldn't hear my own voice."

Gods! Even now, when I'd been seeking control, I'd

affected others around me. I pulled him close. We shifted so I could get next to him, pressing him tight to me.

He held me for a while before whispering, "I take it that didn't go well?"

"I found the silence," I said, trembling. "But I never want to go back there."

"Oh?"

"That's... that's where I went when I was dying, after fighting Dantoine. It's a gaping void, full of nothingness. I... I think that's where I found my powers?" I wasn't sure, it was just a hunch, but it seemed right. "But... it terrifies me. I don't want to go back."

Daz held me closer.

"I..." He hesitated, stuttering with a few more false starts, unable to express himself. Whatever he was about to say... he was thinking it through. Finally, he sighed and said it. "Which do you fear more: affecting others, or that void?"

Ah, yes, I could see why he might have hesitated. Not an easy question to ask and even harder to answer, putting me on the spot.

I took strength from the fact that he thought me strong enough to face that question.

So... which *did* I fear more?

I pushed back from him as I considered this.

My powers were wild, free, uncontrolled. I wasn't so much scared of my powers, as much as the unknown of what they *might* do, which was terrifying. The trouble was, my powers were more likely to affect those closest to me, as they'd done with Kel during sex and Daz just now.

I didn't want to hurt my guys... but I might, in a fit of anger perhaps.

I sighed.

On the other hand... that dark place within me would hurt no one but me. It was a bridge, a place between life and death and if I wasn't careful, I could lose myself there.

Ultimately, that's what made my choice for me. I'd much rather put myself in danger than those I loved. That's what I'd been doing all my life as a warrior. As much as that void terrified me, it was necessary to face it again.

"I'll go back in," I said, and only then raised my eyes to meet Daz's gaze.

He smiled softly. "I knew you would."

"Better tell me everything now, before I go back in, since I can't seem to hear you when I'm there."

He nodded.

"There isn't much more to it. Once you've mastered the dark, then you bring all your colors into the darkness. For you, it would be silence and song, but the theory is the same. If you can contain your powers in that place, you can then draw them forth when and if you need them, but otherwise they are contained."

Bring my song into the place of silence and contain it, then draw on it when needed... "Got it. Let me try."

He put a hand on my shoulder. "I know you can do it. You're a miracle, Tisi. You always have been. You suddenly blossoming with these powers is just... another facet of your extraordinary nature. I believe in you, Tisera."

I pulled him close once again, holding him as a reward for those touching words. "Thank you."

Then I drew a deep breath and pulled back, ready.

I closed my eyes and sought the darkness, the silence, the void.

It came quickly, as if always there, lurking in the shadows, stalking me. I'd cheated death once, and perhaps it was just a bit annoyed by that.

I quelled my fear as the void took me. I was stronger than this place. I'd survived once and would continue to survive.

I am master here, you hear me? I called out. My voice seemed muted, my shout barely a whisper. That wouldn't do.

I am master here! I said with more force, pulling my powers to me. *I am in control, and you will not take me, I will control you and control my powers!* This time my voice rang out clear, but still not the resounding shout I'd hoped for. I pulled more power and this time I put the words to song:

I am the master here,
Master of song and silence.
From death and dark I take control.
Bow before my dominance!

THE VOID SHUDDERED AND WARPED. I COULDN'T SEE IT, but I felt the shifting of power around me. My voice echoed back to me, full of life and vitality. This was no longer a place of death. I was in control.

Summoning my song, my power, my voice to this place, I poured everything I had into the silence.

And like I had that very first time, music grew.

It began with a hymn. I'd learned — from that first set of meditations with Daz — that hymns were associated with power and spirit, with rulership and creation.

Slowly all the other songs and themes added themselves to the hymn. There came the strong, pulsing cadence of a march, like the very pumping of my heart. A wordless lullaby, soft and sweet, natural and pure. Soaring voices, filled with ardor and energy, joined the chorus while others, low and measured sang counterpoint. The tune of a lively tavern dance added a joyful air to the mix. Then all of these became one, an anthem — *my* anthem — which rose to fill the void.

I opened my eyes slowly, blinking at Daz.

"I think I did it," I whispered.

"I know you did," he said. "I can feel it. You're containing your aura. That and... you... you're practically glowing. It's... I can't... there are no words." Tears welled in his eyes. "You've always been beautiful Tisi, but now you're angelic."

Oh... wow... really?

He smiled, wiping away a tear. "You're the most amazing woman I've ever known," he said, his words touching my heart.

I didn't know what to say, so we sat in silence, simply sharing each other's presence. Then, he cocked his head oddly, as if listening to some distant sound.

"What is it?" I asked.

"I don't know. I sensed... something, but I can't quite figure out what it was."

Before we had time to delve into that, the door burst open.

"The Old Palace is on fire!" Kel huffed, out of breath, from the doorway.

Leo entered behind him and whatever he'd been about to say died on his lips as he looked at me, blinking. "Are you glowing?"

CHAPTER 18

TISERA

I DIDN'T KNOW WHAT TO SAY TO LEO. KEL'S NEWS SEEMED more significant anyway.

"On fire?" I repeated.

My mind hadn't caught on to what that might mean. It wasn't a good thing, but something in Kel's demeanor suggested a deeper significance.

He explained, "We think Prince Victor set the fire as a distraction. Guards and servants are working to put out the flames, but... the Old Palace was mostly wood and it's going up fast. We need everyone around the queen and the royals just in case Victor is about to make his move."

I was up in an instant, ready to do as Kel had suggested, but Daz's next words stopped me.

"No."

We all looked at him.

"He's not going for the queen." Daz got up, all nervous

energy, starting to move. I followed him to the door as he continued. "I felt something a moment ago, and now I know what it was. Veora's aura has vanished. Victor is trying to free her from the dungeons."

Fuck.

None of us questioned Daz on this. We hurried out of the queen's suite to her private audience chamber. Leo quickly explained things to his mother, then we dashed out of her chambers and through the royal wing.

But the dungeons were far below us.

"Why didn't we account for this?" Kel berated himself.

"We did," Leo said. "Veora was well guarded."

Now wasn't the time for second guesses. "Victor may have convinced the guards to let him see her, or he may have a few loyal guards of his own and overpowered the prison guards," I said. "We don't know, and it's no use beating ourselves up for it. At least Veora won't be able to use her power, right Daz?"

He nodded. "They're lost to her for at least a day, hopefully more."

It was a long way down into the dungeons. By the time we got there, the scene was eerily quiet. It was clear Victor had had help. The guards stationed down here had been overwhelmed and slaughtered. Blood splattered the walls and pooled on the floor. Veora's cell was empty, door swinging on creaky hinges.

We were too late.

"Fuck!" I shouted, then took a moment to try to catch my breath.

"I..." Daz shook his head. "Fuck is right. I can't find them. Whatever Veora did to hide Victor's aura... it must be able to hide those near to him as well. I can't sense her. I could try searching for that blank spot, but that's going to get harder and harder as they get farther and farther away."

"Then we do this the old-fashioned way," Kel said, peering at the scene. "There's only one exit from the dungeons. We track their movements from there. See if anyone saw anything or if they've left a trail of blood behind them."

I nodded. He was right.

"Let's go!" And I turned and ran back to the entrance to the dungeons.

As it turned out, Victor's group was fairly easy to track, at least within the palace. Servants remembered the desperately fleeing group. They told us Victor had six guards with him as well as Veora. We also found a few spots where their group had fought and overpowered other guards.

We followed their trail to the palace stables. Eight horses were missing. The group had fought their way out of the main gate, losing three men... but they were in the city now. Yet... where could they go? The city was locked down.

We tried to follow their trail, but the streets of the inner city were busy, and a group of riders wouldn't seem out of place. We asked around, but no one remembered seeing them.

"Still, they can't get out of the city, can they?" Leo asked. We were all a little winded from our frenzied chase.

"They have two options," Daz said, huffing hard.

"They might be able to steal a boat from the docks, or they could hide out and wait for a day or two until Veora gets her powers back, then... she can *fly* them out." Exasperation laced his voice.

I guessed it frustrated him that she knew how to fly and he — with all his powers and knowledge — did not. He knew how to lift and levitate others, but only a few feet, and couldn't seem to do it to himself.

"I'll gather some city guards and do a sweep of the docks," Leo said. "Kel, tell my mother we need to blockade the harbor. It will take a while to set up, and we may be too late, but we have to try."

"No one goes anywhere alone!" I said firmly. "I'll go with Leo, Daz, stay with Kel."

We all agreed to this and split up.

Leo and I gathered as many city guards as we could to do a sweep of the docks but found nothing. As evening fell, the guards kept searching, but Leo and I returned to the palace. There, we found out the situation had gone from bad to worse.

"Eromore has invaded," the queen said, biting off her words. "And Ossara has joined them, crossing our western border."

"Ossara?" I asked confused. I'd known Eromore had been testing our borders, but Ossara had always been a peaceful neighbor.

"Word is that they believe Princes Kira is dead, killed by Victor. They are coming for righteous vengeance."

"But Princess Kira is still alive," I said.

The queen nodded. "It's clear to me now, this was all well-orchestrated in advance. Veora — or Victor as her puppet — was to kill myself and Princess Kira. Thus, weakening us for an invasion from Eromore *and* starting a war with Ossara." She sighed heavily. "We can diffuse the Ossaran threat by sending Kira out to meet them, but she'll need a significant honor guard to ensure she makes it. I have to assume there are spies and assassins all over our countryside right now." She shook her head. "And honestly that will only weaken us against Eromore. We're woefully underprepared for their invasion."

"You have my men," Kel said, stalwart.

"Even buying the services of all the mercenaries in Pearlia, we're still far outmatched," the queen said. "We can hold this city for a time, but..."

"But if they have more like Veora..." I finished for her.

She nodded.

"Then we just have to stop them before they get here," I said firmly.

The queen raised a brow. "I do not doubt your prowess, but you cannot take on an army alone."

"She won't be alone. She'll have me," Leo said drawing up next to me.

The queen shook her head. "No, I will not allow—"

"And she has me," Daz said. "I'll protect them both." He stepped close on my other side.

"As shall I," Kel stated, coming to stand behind us.

"The *four* of you against *forty thousand* men?" the queen scoffed.

"Exactly," I said with a cocky grin. I had the makings of a rough plan in my head. I didn't know if it would work. I gave us a slim chance of success, but if we had enough bravado and bluster... then just maybe... "Leave it to us."

The queen blinked, stunned. "You're insane."

"No," Leo said, his words confident. "She's amazing. I believe in her. She can do anything she puts her mind to."

Hells yeah, I could!

"A Phorasti, a mercenary, a woman warrior, and a prince?" The queen sighed, shaking her head. "I don't know what you have planned, but I'll take anything I can get. Just... don't get my son killed."

It wasn't a resounding endorsement, but I'd take it.

CHAPTER 19

Tɪsᴇʀᴀ

"*Tʜᴀᴛ's ʏᴏᴜʀ ᴘʟᴀɴ?*" Lᴇᴏ sʜᴏᴜᴛᴇᴅ, ᴛʜᴇɴ ǫᴜɪᴇᴛᴇᴅ himself. "I'd never question you in front of my mother, but... Tisi..."

"So, it's a little daring. Aren't you up for some excitement?" My grin might have been a little manic. It was a pretty wild plan.

"It... might work," Daz said slowly. "Providing we get to the Eromorn Army before Victor and Veora; they're the biggest unknown."

Kel shrugged when I looked at him. "It's a hundred percent crazy, but it could work."

My plan was for Daz to disguise us. I'd be Veora, Leo would be Victor. That way the changes wouldn't be too drastic. Daz and Kel wouldn't have to change themselves at all. They'd be our guards. We'd walk right into the Eromorn camp and tell them the real Victor and Veora were fakes. That way, when they arrived, they'd be apprehended and we could take them into custody. After that we just had to escape with them. Also, while we were in the camp we'd do as much damage as we could to sabotage their war effort.

"If they have a Phorasti as strong as me, they might be able to sense the illusion," Daz said softly.

"How likely is that?" I asked.

He shrugged. "They're unlikely to have any Kromasti, like me. But Leo thinks they may have more Ikiosti, like you and Veora. And honestly, I don't know if or how they'll sense things."

"Then I'll be our test. If I can't tell it's an illusion, hopefully none of them will be able to." I didn't know how powerful I was, but Veora had suggested I was more powerful than her, and I had to assume she'd be one of Eromore's more powerful mystics.

Daz nodded. "That could work."

"Then we're set?" I asked.

Leo shook his head, then sighed. "I don't doubt we can do this, but can we take a moment and come up with some contingencies, in case it doesn't work? I just... we'll be in the middle of an enemy camp. If we're found out, we're done for."

He wasn't wrong.

So, we stayed up late into the night planning before we rested.

The next morning, Daz wove the illusions around us, taking his time on the complex shifting of colors, or so he called it. Veora could do this with a kiss — which I found both disgusting and astonishing — demonstrating the vast differences between the two sets of powers.

When he was done, I delved into my newly controlled powers singing various songs to either try to see through the illusion or detect its power around Leo. But my powers didn't seem to be able to penetrate the disguise.

With that, we were set.

Just after noon, hidden under cloaks, we rode out with the large party escorting Princess Kira to the west. Then the four of us broke off from the column, riding hard to the north... to find the advancing Eromorn Army.

We rode as hard as we could, uncertain if Veora and Victor had even escaped the city yet. Daz kept his Phorasti senses up, trying to feel for them, but found nothing.

Armies do not move quickly, and the Eromorn force of nearly fifty thousand men was no exception. But they were well disciplined and as such could travel ten to fifteen miles a day. We met them at the town of Dellhaven, roughly twenty-five miles into Pearlia and fifty miles from the capital. We'd ridden hard and made it by evening. The sky was still light in the west, but the sun had already set.

We paused on a hill south of the town.

"That's... a lot of soldiers," Leo said, voice hushed with awe. Of all of us, he'd never seen a force like this before. It looked like a sea of men, tents, and fires spread over the hills and plains below us.

For me, it looked far too much like the force that had besieged Vestrea, dredging up all sorts of nasty memories. Kel's features hardened, grim. He too must recall those dark days.

When I looked at Daz, he trembled in his saddle. That's when I recalled what he'd told me about his part in the war. His fear was of an entirely different sort, a fear he might have to use his power to kill thousands once again.

"We can do this," I said, though my voice wasn't as strong as I'd hoped it would be. I drew in a long breath, steadying myself then repeated, "We can do this." That sounded better.

Everyone remained tense. I needed another approach.

"I love you all," I said softly. "Whatever happens down there, I... I just wanted to say that you three have made me the happiest woman who ever lived. I wouldn't trade our times together for anything."

"Neither would I," Leo said. "I love you with all my heart and soul."

"I love you with all my heart. And I'm pretty certain my heart is bigger," Kel said, chuckling at his own jibe. Leo laughed as well.

"I love you with all of my being, and you know how powerful my aura is." Daz smiled, having one-upped the other two. They all laughed, some of the tension releasing from them.

Good.

I gave a grim smile. "Let's go be villains." Then I kicked my horse into a canter and proceeded down into the heart of the enemy's forces.

Our first test came as we reached the sentries at the

edge of the camp. We were dressed as we hoped Veora, Victor and their guards would be, in Pearlian armor and attire, but without the tabard and markings of the Pearlian army specifically. Still, we looked like enemies and were quickly stopped.

I summoned all the arrogant bluster I could and shouted at the men, chiding them. "Can't you see who I am?" I sneered, hopefully acting as catty and superior as Veora would. "I'm Veronique de Ouvelas. I've ensorcelled the Crown Prince of Pearlia and brought him as my prize! Now let me pass this instant!"

"I do not know that name," one of the guards called back. According to his rank insignia, this man was a sergeant. "You'll have to come with us, throw down any weapons you have and—"

"Insolent fool!" I shouted at him. "It doesn't matter what you may or may not know. Go and fetch someone important. They will know who I am." That was a gamble, but I had to assume Veora — or Veronique — would be known to *someone* here. It was a risk... but it paid off.

The guards, seeing that we weren't being threatening, other than my vicious words, let us be and the sergeant sent a man running back into the camp.

"We'll see if you are who you claim to be," he called back at me.

Yes... we would indeed see. This would be our first real test of our disguises.

We waited, tension strung tight between my guys and the guards.

The runner returned with a man in his later years,

grey in his hair and beard. He wore some armor, but not full plate. From his rank insignia, he was a general. Good.

He approached, pale blue eyes looking up at me keenly. He studied me for some time before turning to the guards. "Let them pass!" Then he turned to me. "Lady Veronique, if you'd follow me, please."

I resisted the urge to give a petty smile to the guards as we passed. Then I remembered I was playing the part of Veora and did it anyway.

The four of us dismounted, leading our horses as we followed the general.

"It's been a long time," the general said conversationally.

"It has," I said, trying not to say too much and give away that I had no clue who this man might be.

These first few interactions would be the real test. Luckily, we had a few tricks to help us.

His name is Navano Sielnari, Daz's voice spoke into my mind. *He's remembering a dinner with you and other high-ranking members of the army.*

"It was at that dinner, General Sielnari, was it not?" I ventured.

He laughed. "Yes, at Lord Olivan's estate." He looked back at me, those cold blue eyes keen and searching once again. "And what was the name of the fop who drank too much Arani Wine and made a fool of himself?" It was clear he was testing me.

"Lord Esterra," I replied after Daz had divined the answer from searching the general's thoughts once more.

The general nodded. "Yes, yes."

The general didn't quiz me again after that. We

walked through the Eromorn camp as darkness descended over everything. I couldn't help but feel that we'd done it, we'd fooled these people. We were in!

The general led us to a large pavilion. "This is our command tent," he said. "I have a surprise waiting for you inside, my lady."

"A warm bed I hope," I said, joking. I didn't like how he'd said the word *surprise*.

He pulled back the tent flap and ushered us through. The room was filled with high ranking Eromorn soldiers. And there, standing next to a large table strewn with maps and notes, were Veora and Victor.

Well, fuck.

CHAPTER 20

"IMPOSTER!" I CRIED OUT, HOPING IF I GOT THERE FIRST IT might cause some confusion.

Veora said nothing, she simply smiled as if she had everything under control.

"Indeed." The general nodded as he entered and moved to stand between us and the others who looked like us. "*One* of you *is* an imposter. But you have both passed my tests. So... how should I determine which of you is which?" He eyed both of us.

Interesting. I might still have a chance to fool him and turn the tables on Veora.

Yet she replied before I could speak. "Simple, my dear Navano. Take each of us to your bed. One of us knows exactly what you like, the other... will be raped by you." Veora gave me that superior cat-like grin. "One of us doesn't care who we fuck, the other just might. Isn't that right, Tisi?"

The general looked at me with a feral smile, as if he wanted to devour me. "I'm sure, Lady Veronique, you recall how we spent that night at Lord Olivan's Estate?"

Do I want to know? I asked Daz in my head.

You really don't. The general has rather deviant and violent tastes.

Fuck.

Yeah.

What do we do now? I asked.

Plan G.

He'd be saying that to Leo and Kel as well, warning them of our next move. I silently thanked Leo, who'd made us spend all that time coming up with contingencies. Veora being here had ruined our original plan and our first five alternates.

Leo, Kel, and I dove for cover as Daz filled the room with fire.

Which was almost instantly extinguished.

"How...?" Daz whispered.

Then I caught the unmistakable sound of Veora's haughty laughter. "Master Phorasti, may I introduce *my* master in the arcane arts."

I rose to my knees to see the man who strode forward. He was tall and rake-thin, with gaunt, yellow-grey skin stretched over sharp features and long, bone-white hair. He smiled, a horrid rictus thing revealing rotting teeth.

When he spoke, his voice was soft and raspy, as if half-dead already. "I've always wanted to test my abilities against a Master Kromasti. It seems, my wish has finally come true."

Fuck and double-fuck. How were we going to get out of this? We didn't have a plan for a half-dead, super-powerful Ikiosti.

It was time to improvise. "Daz, can you take him?"

"I—"

"Good, do that. Leo, take Victor. Veora is mine. Kel, you have... everyone else. Go!"

"Wait, *everyone else*?" Kel shouted back at me as the room erupted into chaos.

Luckily, our little ruse had allowed us to keep our weapons. Also, I was a bit more prepared than most of the fights I'd been in recently. The dress I wore — to play the part of Veora — lay over a chain-mail shirt, which would protect my torso and upper arms. Next to me, Leo carried two swords and as he drew one, I took the other. It wasn't much, but it was better than a dagger and no armor. And going against Veora — or Veronique — who didn't seem to have either, I liked my odds.

I launched myself at her, vaulting onto the large table. Yet, even as I did, she shot up into the air, flying. It seemed Daz's suppression of her powers had worn off. She drew out a dagger, to cut the heavy canvas of the tent and escape into the night.

I wasn't about to let that happen. I might not be able to fly, but I reached down into my soul, finding my powers, and summoned the power of a march to strengthen myself, then I leaped high into the air and slashed at her.

She left off cutting the tent, using her dagger to parry

my thrust. But the strike had been a feint. Instead, I used my free hand to grab her other arm, then I surged my powers to ensure I wouldn't let go.

Instantly, she knew what I was doing. I'd gotten ahold of her. She'd not be able to escape without taking me with her.

Panic surged in her eyes.

I grinned. "I've got you now," I whispered and slashed again.

CHAPTER 21

Leonin

I DOVE AND ROLLED UNDER THE LONG TABLE, EVEN AS Veora flew away. I came up on the other side in the spot she'd left, beside my brother.

He'd had enough time to draw his sword, and our two blades crossed with a clash of steel. The rest of the room around us erupted into chaos and magic, but they avoided us for the most part.

"I don't want to hurt you, brother. You may have been training with Tisera, but I'll bet I'm still better with a sword than you are. Surrender now, and I give you my word you'll be treated well."

"Can you even hear yourself?" I asked with a shake of my head. "Look at where you are. You're in an enemy command post, surrounded by those who wish to overthrow *our* kingdom."

Victor smiled and laughed. "Overthrow? No. We'll

make sure Mother is out of the way, then the kingdom will fall to its rightful heir: me."

"You really think Eromore will let you live? You'll be dead the instant Mother is gone. Why would they want you as a ruler when they could take Pearlia for themselves?"

A glimmer of doubt shaded his eyes. Veora's control over him wasn't complete... but it was enough to quell that moment of hesitation. "No, you're wrong. Veora loves me. She'll be my queen and—"

"And Ossara will invade. They're already coming, allied with Eromore. Part of Veora's plan was to kill Kira and incite Ossara to war. You're a pawn, brother, you've always been. Please, let's get out of here and go home!" I caught another flash of uncertainty, but my words weren't enough to sway him. Instead, his doubt turned to anger.

"Enough!" he hissed and attacked.

This was no longer the Victor I knew. I wouldn't reach him with words... and he was right, if we fought with blades, he'd win.

Unless...

I'd caught some of Tisi's work with Victor during her palace trainer test. And, as I'd hoped, Victor initiated with his signature: beat, feint, lunge combo, which Tisi had scolded him for. I was ready for it, and I stepped away from his lunge, knocking his sword down with all my strength. I quickly followed up by stepping on his sword, which pulled it from his hand, and it clattered to the ground. I slid my foot back, kicking his sword away from him, then sheathed my own blade.

"Let's fight like men," I said, raising my fists.

Fear flickered behind his eyes, something I'd never seen in all the times we'd sparred. He knew I'd been training in hand-fighting and that *I* now had the upper hand.

He didn't attack. He raised his fists and waited for me to come to him. Smart. Apparently, I'd told him a bit too much of my training and how I'd gotten really good at turning an opponent's attack against them.

I tested his defenses with a couple quick jabs. He backed off and dodged, instead of trying to parry. He looked around, desperate to find anything that might help him. His gaze settled on the sheathed sword at my hip.

I punched again. This time he took the hit, reaching for my blade. I quickly followed up my punch with a knee to his groin.

Sorry brother, but you have three kids, so hopefully if I did any permanent damage down there, you'll have them at least.

He doubled over with a grunt, releasing my blade. I had him now. I grabbed one of his arms, while he was distracted, then quickly stepped behind him locking the arm in place.

"You're coming with me, and we're getting you out of here," I hissed in his ear.

"Fuck you, Leo! I'll never—"

I jammed his arm up farther.

Just to be sure he'd be compliant, I drew in close behind him and put my other arm around his neck, choking him. I didn't want to knock him out entirely, only weaken him.

He struggled, elbowing me in the ribs with his free

arm. I'd have a hell of a bruise in that spot tomorrow, but I kept my hold on him as I backed us slowly toward the tent's exit.

I had a moment then, to take in the fight around us.

Tisi hung from Veora. She'd lost her sword and the two of them struggled for control of a single dagger.

Daz and the elder Ikiosti traded blasts of mystical energy, both looking like they'd met their match.

Kel moved so fast it was hard to see his blade as he battled all the others in the command tent. But he bled from several deep wounds, his movements starting to slow. And as much as he'd tried to occupy everyone else in the tent, a small group had been watching Victor and me. Now that I'd won that fight, they closed in.

"Kel, let's get out of here!" I called.

"Not without Tisi!" he shouted back.

He was right. As much as I wanted to flee, I couldn't leave Tisera behind. But with Victor still struggling in my arms, I was virtually helpless against these new attackers.

Victor rasped a chuckle. "You may have beaten me, brother, but you've lost. Give up."

That was not going to happen.

But still, I could see no way out of this.

It would take a miracle.

CHAPTER 22

Kelric

I had trained relentlessly all my life. I was a consummate warrior. I'd faced hundreds, if not thousands of men trying to kill me and lived to tell of it. But this fight was proving to be my most challenging.

Never before had I gone against so many foes alone. I had no one to help me, the others were all occupied. I had to win this impossible fight on my own, because Tisi had told me to, and because if I didn't, it would cost me my life.

So, I fought through pain and doubt and the impossibility of my situation and simply focused on one man... then the next.

I heard Leo's cry for help and a part of me knew he was right. I should help him, and we should be fleeing. But if we did, that would leave all these men to focus on Daz or Tisi, and I wouldn't allow that.

I didn't know how many men I'd killed so far. I couldn't think of that. I had to focus on those in front of me.

Three men approached. One stayed where he was, while the other two spread out around me, trying to form a triangle. I couldn't let them surround me.

I surged toward the one on my left and knocked his sword aside, then hacked down into his neck with a roar. I spun back to the others as that man fell, but I hadn't been fast enough. The man who had been on my right had charged in. I tried to block his strike, but he still managed a shallow slice through my armor. Another wound among many. I'd lost count. I gritted my teeth at this new pain, trying to ignore it. Eventually my body would either collapse from fatigue or blood loss, but I vowed to keep fighting until that happened.

Two on one, they attacked in intervals, not at the same time, smart. It meant I was having to work twice as hard to keep from getting hit. And half-a-dozen additional men — if not more — waited, inching forward, looking for an opening, ready to kill me if these ones failed.

I allowed a hit to slip through, I had to in order to follow up as the one man withdrew. He wasn't expecting that and died quickly. I had tried to get out of the way of the other man who I'd allowed to strike me, but not enough.

Another wound.

My left leg was starting to go numb, slower, sluggish. But I was quick enough to cut down the last man with ease.

The next set didn't rush in right away. I didn't know what I looked like, but there was fear written on their features: fear and... the faint hope of victory. If they kept me occupied long enough, I'd succumb to my wounds.

But not yet.

I roared at them and was grimly satisfied as they all flinched back. I used that moment's hesitation and charged them. I took out one before he regained himself. But the group spread out after that, moving away from me, around me.

I could see their plan. Just keep me caged in, moving with me — slow as I was now — until I wore myself out and collapsed. They surrounded me, making sure I had no way out, while keeping their distance.

"You've failed," one of them sneered at me.

He died — very surprised — with my sword in his chest. I'd thrown the weapon. Then, I charged through the gap that had made, plucking up my sword as I passed. After that, I put my back to the canvas of the tent, making sure they couldn't get behind me.

"I'm not dead yet," I croaked out, voice nowhere near as threatening as I'd hoped it would be. I was utterly exhausted and out of breath. "Come at me!"

"Why?" one said. "We just have to wait until you die. It's you who have to come at us." He wore a superior smile.

He was still wearing that smile when a gout of flame incinerated him... and several others.

"Thanks, Daz," I whispered.

There were only a few left, five or six, maybe a few more? I wasn't sure, my vision was blurring and my mind hazy. Still, Daz had given me an opening and I took advantage of it. I roared to give myself the strength I needed — the last of my strength — and charged among them.

I wasn't dead yet, and I'd keep fighting until they were all dead or I was. Those were my choices: Fight or die.

I chose to fight.

CHAPTER 23

DAZAR

I HOPED HELPING KEL WOULDN'T COST ME MY FIGHT.

The Ikiosti Master was powerful and relentless. Never before had I faced an opponent so well matched against me. Any distraction might cost me, but I'd felt Kel's aura fluctuate, and sensed there were far too many men around him. So, I risked an attack to help Kel, reducing the number of men around him to less than ten. I hoped he could handle them.

But as I'd feared, the Ikiosti Master used my brief lapse in attention to strike. I'd had physical defenses prepared, but he must have sensed them and attacked my mind instead, stunning me. I surged blue and green to clear my mind, but that was another moment I wasn't focused on this infuriating Ikiosti. He took that time to attack my spirit, sucking the very essence out of me, weakening my resolve.

He was a true master, cunning and quick, using all the power he possessed in curious and beguiling ways to tear at me from every angle. Yet again, I cursed the masters at the White Tower for not teaching us more about Ikiosti... specifically how to fight them! Their powers were more subtle and hidden than ours, and I was finding out just how much of a problem that could be.

I surged violet for my spirit, but that only seemed to feed into his drain on me, sucking my essence faster.

I fell to my knees, body growing weak as my spirit failed.

An immense pressure crushed my mind, body, and soul all at once. I was a bug and he squashed me under his heal. He laughed, sensing his victory.

But I couldn't die, not while Tisi needed me. I would never leave her. Our love gave me strength in the darkest of times, and I surged that strength now, to resist the Ikiosti.

And with the next — fading — beat of my heart, I knew what I needed to do.

Surging red, the color of love and strength, I shot to my feet and launched myself at the aging Ikiosti. I hoped he'd not be expecting a purely physical attack.

He wasn't.

I bowled into him, feeling frail bones break as I tackled him to the floor. I punched his face, feeling his jaw skew, but alas, that was as far as I got before he regained himself enough to blast Phora at me. I was thrown off him, landing hard on my back several feet away.

I rose slowly, seeing my foe do the same. We were both worn and weary.

I reached out to his fluctuating aura and tried to suppress his powers, as I'd done with Veora. But even as I did, I felt a similar suppression on my aura as well. We were both trying to take the other's power.

The question was: who was stronger? Who would last longer?

It quickly became apparent: it wouldn't be me. I might have been a master, but this Ikiosti had had many more years to perfect his craft and build his power. I was almost as strong as he was... but not as experienced.

And I couldn't even call out for help. Even that much of a lapse in my concentration and he'd crush me.

I'd lost.

And that's when a dagger hurtled down and plunged itself into the Ikiosti's throat.

He died instantly.

I looked up to see Tisi winking down at me.

Then Veora blasted her with a Phora-empowered shout. Tisi was sent flying, crashing through a sturdy tent-post, before slamming into the ground.

CHAPTER 24

Tisera

I had enough battle-instinct to roll and try to come to my feet just in case there was a follow-up attack. Still, my head spun and my back ached, both from crashing through that sturdy pole and hitting the ground.

And I'd lost hold of Veora. She'd be able to get away now.

But she didn't flee.

My vision cleared enough for me to see the scene. Daz was down, looking exhausted, trying to stand but unable. Kel fought, despite far too much blood flowing out of him, and he still faced half a dozen men. Even as I watched, he fell to one knee, unable to keep moving. Leo stood by the exit, holding his brother by the neck, surrounded by four men moving in slowly.

As for me, I was winded and aching, but far from out

of this fight. I'd spent a lot of energy clinging onto Veora to keep her from escaping, while fighting for control of her dagger. I'd finally managed to get it off her, only to see Daz locked in a struggle with the Ikiosti Master. So, I'd thrown the weapon, instead of using it on Veora.

That meant Veora was also mostly healthy. She also surveyed the scene and reassessed things. That feral smile of hers spread on her face, eyes glinting. Instead of fleeing, she went on the offensive.

Her first attack was on Daz, stunning him. I didn't see it but felt her use her powers. Daz gripped his head, trying to shake off whatever she'd done.

I was torn. I should help Kel or Leo, but if I didn't deal with Veora, she'd be a wild card that could easily dominate this fight.

"Fuck!" I swore.

I ran toward Veora, plucking up the dagger from the neck of the Ikiosti Master on my way. I threw it again, taking out one of the men closing in on Kel. Then I leaped, using my powers to enhance my strength once more.

Veora was expecting me and deftly floated out of the way of my attempt to grab her. Yet I'd positioned myself so that if I didn't get her, I'd come down behind the men moving in on Leo. I snapped the neck of one man as I landed, then kicked out at the man next to him, breaking his leg. That left Leo with two, I hoped he could take them.

I turned back to Veora, who looked enraged at what I'd been able to do.

"No!" she screamed, and a wave of power emanated

from her.

I summoned my powers — a combination of a battle-hymn and an aria — and managed to block Veora's blast. Everyone else in the tent was blown to the ground.

The tent itself buckled as another pole collapsed. With two poles gone, the remaining supports began to fall under the weight of the heavy canvas. At the same time, several lanterns, knocked over by Veora's blast, spilled oil, beginning fires throughout the area.

The falling fabric forced Veora to the ground. But it also obscured my sight of her. So, I rushed to Leo, who was close to an exit. I tackled him and Prince Victor out of the command tent as it settled to the ground.

"Sorry," I said, seeing him wince as I got off him.

Leo had a good hold on Victor, who seemed mostly insensate. I wasn't worried the crown prince would get away. "I'll be okay," Leo grunted, clearly not okay. "Save the others and kill that bitch!"

Leo's language surprised me. He didn't use words like that often.

"Take care of yourself," I whispered. "We're still in the middle of an enemy camp." And the glamor Daz had put on me and Leo had worn off.

"I'll hide. I know you can find me. Just... survive this."

"I will." I leaned down to kiss his cheek then grabbed his sword and rose, returning to the mostly flattened command tent. Those oil fires hadn't been completely extinguished by the heavy cloth and several areas of canvas were blackening, starting to smolder as the fire burned through. This entire area would be ablaze soon.

The three men who'd been close to Leo and the exit

were still struggling to get out. One had reached the flap and was just starting to rise. I didn't have time for mercy, and I couldn't let him rouse the rest of the camp. He lost his head with a single swipe of Leo's sword.

I gritted my teeth.

I hated this.

I'd wanted to leave death behind me. The years of peace, learning to use my skills in other ways, meant I'd grown to abhor war. I didn't want to kill anyone, but these men were the commanders. Their deaths now meant many other — mostly innocent — foot soldiers wouldn't have to die later.

Eromore had started this war, but I intended to finish it, here and now.

So, as much as I hated myself for it, I needed to make sure no commanders survived the night. The other two men, still struggling under the heavy canvas to get to the exit, were given a quick death. I steeled myself and cringed at the necessity.

There weren't many others left, and they weren't near an exit, which meant I had a moment. I wanted to go after Veora, but a fire was spreading quickly, near where Daz was trapped under the tent. I knew exactly where he was. His aura called to me. I ran over to cut him free of the fabric.

Daz groaned, still clutching his head. Whatever Veora had done was still affecting him. I scooped him up, carrying him away from the burgeoning flames.

As I walked, I used my powers to examine what afflicted him. I found discord, like a jagged crown, around his head. I tried to soothe it away, but Veora must have poured a lot of power into this disabling attack as I couldn't easily dispel it.

I set Daz down away from the tent and focused, seeking deeper into this strange effect. This time, I sensed what I'd missed before, a thread of a whisper, keeping the true power behind the attack hidden. Knowing that, I whispered a mixed tune: mostly lullaby with a metered madrigal and a march.

The jagged song of pain and confusion broke and faded from around Daz.

"You well?" I asked,

He sighed heavily. "I'll live, but I'm beat."

"Then rest. I'll return for you."

He didn't even speak, just went limp as he nodded.

I rose and sought out with my powers again. I found Kel's unique song, though it was so very weak. Around him were others, the remaining commanders. I sensed Veora too, crawling toward the edge of the tent. There was time enough to help Kel and deal with the commanders before I had to think about Veora again.

Sprinting over, I stabbed down through the heavy canvas to take out the last of the officers. Then I cut away the cloth around Kel. I didn't even try to move him. I just touched his face and pushed as much of a healing song into him as I could. Only as I began to grow faint, did I recall Daz's warning about healing: that it could kill the healer if the person's wounds were too grave. I tore my hand away from Kel's cheek with a gasp as I swooned and fell over.

I couldn't breathe, gasping for air. I managed one full breath and then simply lay there trying to steady my breathing as I blinked away the darkness at the edges of my vision. That had been a bit too close. Kel would survive, even if he was still gravely wounded. He was unconscious and helpless, but still I had to leave him. I needed to get to Veora before she escaped.

Yet even as I rose — unsteady — Veora wormed her way out from under the canvas. She leaped to her feet and fled.

"No," I gasped and forced myself to go after her, staggering on watery limbs, my head spinning.

"Fuck." How could I face her like this?

I didn't have an answer, but I couldn't let her escape. I summoned my powers — now seriously depleted — and gave myself a little bit of a healing lullaby, while adding a march for strength. Then I used that power to charge off into the night after Veora.

I caught up with her as we reached the edge of the camp. The command tents were at the rear of the encampment. Beyond them lay open fields and rolling hills.

"Veora!" I called out. She was still a dozen paces away.

She spun at my voice, fear in her eyes as she turned back. But quickly that fear turned to arrogance. She could see how weak I was. She hadn't been using her powers to run, and I had. I was exhausted and she was still mostly fresh.

She laughed. "Oh... Tisi, my dear, what have you done? Given yourself to me on a platter, have you? Foolish girl."

She summoned her power.

I summoned — what remained of — mine.

This was it.

One of us would die here.

CHAPTER 25

Tisera

Despite my exhausted state, I had a plan for this fight. My Phora was drained and my strength waning, but I was still willing to bet I could take Veora in hand-to-hand combat. So, I put all of my Ikiosti powers into strengthening myself, instilling strength and vigor with an aria-march. Then I launched myself bodily at Veora.

She waved her hand in front of her and I collided with a barrier before I hit her.

"Oh, Tisi, you're so predictable. Of course you'd try to defeat me physically," Veora chided, then laughed. "And I'm more than willing to test my combat skills against yours, but let's get things solidly in my favor first, shall we?"

I didn't like the sound of that.

When I tried to move around the invisible shield before me, I found one to my right, then another to my left. I tried to leap up, but only bashed my head into an invisible barrier above me.

Veora laughed.

"Oh, it's so much fun to watch you struggle." Her vicious smile contorted into a face-twisting sneer.

"Little Tisi, blessed with so much strength and power. You were given everything, even your three lovers. I had to scrape and claw for scraps, paying for my power with my body and soul. I will so enjoy watching you die. I may not be as strong as you, but you've clearly not learned to moderate your powers. This box you're in will steal your air and doesn't even require that much strength to maintain. You'll slowly die in there, and when you're nice and weak, I'll finish you off myself."

Fuck!

She was right. I hadn't learned to moderate my powers, *and* I'd rushed in without much of a plan. Now I was trapped.

There was only one option left to me.

I began to act like I was choking, losing air. I wasn't, not yet, even though the air grew thin. I subsumed my Ikiosti powers back into me. There wasn't much left, but I balled what remained into a tight reserve to use later. That meant my body was instantly weak and weary once again. I collapsed, not having to fake that, even as I clutched at my throat.

This new plan hinged entirely on being able to fool someone who'd spent their life fooling others. I wasn't sure if it would work...

But then I saw the gleam of victory in Veora's eyes.

She bought my act, believed it because she wanted to believe she could defeat me.

I fake-struggled a bit longer before slowly stilling my movements, making convulsive-gasping motions with my whole body. Even as I feigned air-loss the last of the air in this limited space faded away. If she kept it up much longer, I really would choke and die.

Veora laughed triumphantly and released the box around me. The night's breeze washed over me. Still, I kept my breaths shallow, playing dead.

Veora came to me, crouching and putting a knee on my throat as she stroked my hair. "This is how you die, Tisi. Looking up at me. Isn't that wonderful?"

I had thought she'd try to strangle me with her hands, not this. Now I truly couldn't breathe, and I wouldn't be able to do much to her. She was at an odd angle, and I was too weak.

Luckily, I'd studied that disabling spell she'd put on Daz so I could undo it. I summoned what little power I had left and pushed it at her in a similar mind-splintering way. Since my power was so reduced, it wouldn't affect her for long, but it did stun her. She fell back, releasing my neck.

I pounced.

Though, I was so fatigued, it was less of a pounce and more of a sluggish flop, but I managed to get on top of her.

I punched her throat. Hopefully that would stun her longer. Then I rolled her over to get an arm around her neck and choke her.

There were two ways to choke someone. The proper

way would knock them out without killing them. The other way could easily kill them. In the back of my head, I knew I was doing it wrong, but I didn't care. Veora was too troublesome to let live.

She struggled beneath me.

Her powers lashed out at me, trying to stun or harm me.

She blasted my mind. All my thoughts vanished. I didn't know who I was, but I knew I couldn't let go of this woman.

Pain lanced through my entire body as she bashed me and burned me. Skin seared, bones broke. Yet I used the last of my strength to keep hold of her.

Veora ripped at my very soul, but still I wouldn't relent. This woman was a festering wound upon the world. I'd ensure she caused no more pain.

Slowly... very slowly... her powers waned and her body stilled. Yet even after she went limp, I didn't let up. I'd fooled her by doing something similar. I wouldn't fall for the same ruse. I choked her until my own strength gave out, and my arms went watery and limp. Then I finally released her and rolled off.

Veora didn't move.

I was too weary and broken to smile.

I didn't know I'd fallen asleep until light stabbed my eyes and I came awake slowly, still utterly enfeebled and exhausted.

I groaned.

Rolling my head to one side, I saw Veora still there... dead.

That gave me a hint of strength, partly from knowing

I'd defeated her, and partly from not wanting to lie next to a corpse.

It took a long time — and every ounce of strength and resolve I had — to sit up. Not only was I weak and worn out, but Veora had done a good job of breaking my body. Debilitating pain, from dozens of wounds, made it difficult to move at all.

Still, I gasped and gritted my teeth as I forced myself upright.

Dizziness swept over me, but I clenched my eyes shut and breathed through it.

If sitting had taken forever, trying to get to my feet seemed an eternity of agony and disorientation. And that only got me to one knee.

I don't know how I managed to get to my feet, only that I found myself stumbling along, one tiny step at a time, sometime later.

When I looked back... I hadn't gone far.

"There you are!"

I turned at the familiar voice. My mind was so addled I didn't recognize it, I didn't even recognize the fuzzy image of a man heading for me. But then, as he drew closer, he came into focus.

Daz.

"I've got you," he whispered, putting strong, supportive arms around me. I leaned heavily on him with a sigh. I couldn't move another step. When he realized that, Daz swept me into his arms.

"We're still..." I couldn't finish, talking was too hard.

"In the middle of an enemy camp," he said, voice low. "Yeah, I know, but no one knows what happened or who we are. I commandeered one of the command tents and hid Leo, Kel, and Victor in there. From what I understand, no commanders survived the night. Some of the camp is breaking and preparing to leave, but most of the rest is just milling around confused."

"That wo—" I couldn't even get out two words this time.

"Won't last long? Yeah, I know. But hopefully long enough for you to regain your strength a little. Here we are."

He slid into a large tent and laid me beside Kel on a bed. Leo was awake and keeping his eyes on a bound and gagged Victor. Seeing me, Leo rose and came over.

"How are you?" he asked me, then immediately turned to Daz. "How is she?"

"Weak and broken," Daz said. I let him speak for me. "It looks like she defeated Veora, but I'm guessing it took everything she had." That summed it up.

"Can you...?" Leo asked, looking at me. From that worried gaze I surmised I looked about as good as I felt.

"Heal her? No," Daz said. "I'm still weak as it is and... somehow... despite all her wounds, I sense no impending danger of death. Tisi is strong. She'll survive this."

It didn't feel that way, but I trusted Daz.

I gave Leo a weak smile. "Yup," I managed to say.

Leo kissed me softly. "Then rest." He half-laughed. "Let us protect you for once."

I closed my eyes with a faint smile and sank back into the dark abyss of sleep.

I woke to distant shouts and calls of alarm.

I still felt groggy and weak and far too injured but had

regained some tiny measure of strength. I rolled my head to the side, to better see what was happening.

Daz stood by the tent flap peeking out. I must have groaned as he looked back at me. "Something's happening. We may need to flee soon. Can you walk?" I didn't even say anything before he tilted his head observing me. "Probably not."

I shrugged and even that small motion took a lot out of me.

Leo was next to me in an instant. He helped me — so very gentle yet firm — sit up. Still, I panted and grimaced from pain and fatigue having done that much.

I looked at Kel, still out cold.

"What about him?" At least I could manage full sentences now.

"Still very hurt," Daz said. "I added a bit of healing to what you'd given him, but he'll not be able to walk any time soon." Daz looked around as if trying to find some answer to our predicament inside this tent.

That's when we heard it... distant sounds... of fighting.

CHAPTER 26

D AZAR

"S TAY HERE , I'M GOING TO TAKE A LOOK ," I SAID TO L EO and Tisi. "I'll be careful, don't worry." I knew they'd worry, but hopefully I wouldn't be gone long.

I slipped out of the tent and into the late-morning sun. There wasn't much action around me, the command area of the camp was mostly deserted.

My powers were still recovering from last night's ordeal. After Tisi had rescued me — dispelling that strange mind-affecting spell upon me — I'd rested, doing a few of my meditations to help recover.

When I'd finally stood, I'd seen Kel not far away and a burning command tent, with flames closing in on him.

Despite the command area being removed from the main camp, the large fire had brought men running. I'd shouted to some of them a sneak attack, that the Pearlians were fleeing into the night. A few had remained to put out the fire, others had gone in search of the phantom force.

Luckily, no one questioned who *I* was.

I'd surged my strength to carry Kel — a heavy man in heavier armor — to another tent and safety, then had gone in search of Leo and Tisi.

Leo had dragged his brother to another of the commander's tents. I found them both out cold and carried them to the tent with Kel.

But that had exhausted me. I'd tried to go after Tisi, but after one step had fallen on my face and slept till dawn.

That's when I'd gone and found Tisi, looking like she'd been trampled by a herd of horses, yet somehow stumbling along, averse to death.

Veora's corpse hadn't been far away. I'd double-checked her aura to ensure she was dead. She was. Had been for hours. Which meant she'd lied to me when she'd said Prince Victor would die if she did. Thank the gods for that.

After I'd carried Tisi back to our hide-out, I'd rested again, meditating and eating a little from the stores in this tent. The commanders had been well provisioned.

As it was, I had enough in me now to summon my colors for a long-distance observational spell. I sought out with my senses to the thousands of auras around me, focusing on the direction I heard fighting.

I got a pretty decent picture of what was happening. A small force, perhaps five-hundred men on horseback, swept through the Eromorn camp. I guessed the queen had sent a scouting force, to see what our little band had been able to accomplish, and the commander of the cavalry had seen the disarray of the enemy camp and decided to attack.

The men on horseback easily overpowered the confused and unprepared Eromorn men. I reached out to the Pearlian troops and used up most of the power I'd regained that morning by sending a command for them to leave off their foray and circle the camp to us.

They wouldn't know why they were coming, but they'd find us soon enough.

I returned to the tent.

"Leo, get out there, a force of Pearlian cavalry is on its way. You're recognizable, so flag them down and let them know we need help. I'll look after Victor."

Leo didn't question my command and was quickly out of the tent.

"Thank the gods," Tisi breathed.

I felt the same.

Knowing it wouldn't take much for me to simply cling to a rider on horseback, I used what remained of my power to heal Kel a bit more. His wounds wouldn't fare well if he was flopped over the back of a horse. He stirred and woke as I nearly collapsed.

Good. Hopefully he'd be able to ride now.

Leo returned with several knights not too long after that. The five of us were placed on mounts and quickly taken away from the Eromorn camp, leaving it in chaos.

We arrived at the capital as another force rode out, five or six thousand men, probably every soldier Pearlia could muster.

Victor was given over to the palace guards and watched around the clock.

The rest of us collapsed into sleep.

Several days later, news came that the leaderless Eromorn army had been routed and was returning home, defeated by a force a fraction of their size. That same day, word came from the west that the Ossarans had met with Princes Kira and turned back as well.

Pearlia was saved.

TISI, KEL, AND I CONVALESCED IN LEO'S SUITE, STAYING IN the palace. Leo came and went, bringing food and news and the occasional visitor. Princes Alice and Tisi's Aunt Emri came most often.

During one of these visits, as Tisi chatted with the two other women, Leo pulled me aside. "My mother wishes to see you, when you're feeling up to it," he said softly.

I grimaced.

"She seems... apologetic," he said by way of mediation. "It's not an emotion expressed by the queen very often. Now might be the best time to speak with her."

I nodded. "Thank you, I will," I said. Since I was mostly recovered, I saw no need to wait. "I'll go now."

Leo nodded, and I left.

I was admitted into the queen's private audience chamber where I bowed and was told to rise.

"Thank you for coming, Master Phorasti," the queen said, voice tempered.

I rose and tried to suppress the agitation I still felt whenever I looked at her. She'd been going to use me as a weapon of war. I still resented her for that.

"What is it Your Majesty desires?" I said, voice cool.

"To release you from the bonds I had placed on you previously." She sighed. "I... was wrong to use you like that. I'm... sorry." She did seem genuinely apologetic.

I sighed, and with it, tried to release my anger. "Thank you, Your Majesty. Is that all?"

She shook her head. "No. I will not compel you, Master Phorasti, but I have a request for you to consider."

"I'm listening."

"Can you... return Prince Victor to how he was?" Her façade broke: no longer the strong and indominable queen, just a lost and worried mother. It lasted only an instant before *the queen* returned. "Is that within your power?"

"I honestly don't know, Your Majesty. The powers used on him are far different than my own. I may not be able to help him, but... I will try, that is something I am willing to do for the crown." I quickly added, "But... if I do this, the crown will owe *me* a favor," I said. "Anything I ask."

The queen nodded. "If you return my Victor to me, as he was, then anything in my power is yours to have."

I hadn't really expected her to agree so easily. I nodded. "Is that all?"

"Yes, you may go."

I turned, but before I reached the door I stopped and looked back. "If Tisera were to help me restore Victor to himself, would that favor extend to her as well?"

The queen nodded. "Yes, of course."

I nodded and left.

We didn't start our work on Victor right away. Knowing it would be a grueling process, I waited for Tisi and I to be fully recovered before we began. Then followed weeks of arduous work undoing the months of manipulations Veora had placed on Prince Victor.

The trouble wasn't removing thoughts or feelings, so much as removing the *right* ones. The prince's mission had been to kill his mother and take the throne. Veora had built that on some existing hostility and resentment toward the queen. We had to carefully remove only what she'd added. Hence, the work was painstakingly slow, finding the subtle weave of unnaturalness to some thoughts and feelings.

I worked at a high level, gently massaging the prince's aura. Tisi's job was much harder. Since she had Ikiosti powers like Veora, she could delve deeper, listening to the song of the prince's soul and slowly shifting it back to what it had been. We rarely left the prince's side. Spare beds were brought so we could remain close to him when we rested.

As we worked, I taught her more about her powers. Though, I also learned as much as I taught. I could help her with generalities around control and manipulation of the ability, while she taught me about the specific songs and the intricate use of each. There was a lot of confusion, trying to translate colors into songs, but after months of working together we came to know each other's powers very well.

After two months, we were nearly finished. Tisi did

all the work now. I remained close to her, giving her energy and healing when she needed it. Victor himself was mostly conscious these days, trying to help where he could as he regained more of himself.

One morning I woke to hear soft voices nearby. Tisi spoke quietly to Victor. They sat, chairs pulled close together, near the fire, away from the small sitting area in the room. I listened in on their conversation as I slowly came to consciousness.

"...good, Kira agrees on all those points. It sounds like you're nearly there," Tisi said. Then, a bit more hesitantly. "Kira would... like to see you, if you're ready?"

Victor sighed heavily. "The things I did to her and my children..."

"They know it wasn't you."

"That's just it! A part of it *was* me," Victor bit out, sounding angry at himself. "I love Kira, but a part of me had always resented our political marriage." He sighed. "I wasn't always the best husband and father to them, even before all of this."

"And now?"

Victor's voice was heavy with emotion. He sounded like he was weeping. "I want to be the man they deserve."

"Then it's time you told them that."

I didn't see it, but I assumed Victor nodded.

Tisi finished with, "Good, I'll let them know."

I caught sight of her as she stood then stretched; lithe and perfect. I smiled. It felt like the first time in ages that I had. A spark of joy bloomed in my soul. I was so very lucky to know this beautiful and powerful woman.

Tisi spied me watching her and put a bit more

emphasis into her stretch, pushing out her breasts and swaying her hips a little as she winked at me. My smile grew at her playful display. She was my home, my life, my joy, and my love. And far more than all of that... miraculously, she loved me in return.

That night we returned to Leo's rooms, and I asked Kel and Leo if I could have her to myself. The two men agreed.

Tisi and I lay, holding each other close. There were tears and laughs and soft kisses, nothing more than that. Tonight was a night to reunite our souls.

"You're the most amazing woman I've ever known," I mumbled as sleep edged upon me. I lay on my back, Tisi on her side next to me, head propped up on one arm.

"You were powerful before all of this and are even more so now. You can fight with your body and your spirit equally. I doubt there has been any woman like you since your goddess Assa walked the earth."

Assa was an Aestrian God, and I didn't know much about her. The Dathi religion was quite different. Still, I'd heard enough about Assa since she was one of the two prime deities of the Aestrian religion. "Wasn't she said to be the epitome of power and womanhood?"

"She was," Tisi said softly. "And I don't think I'm quite a goddess, but... thank you. You have always been there for me, my entire life. You're the most powerful man I know... especially now that I can feel auras." She shook her head, her next words breathed in awe, "I never knew... Well, I knew you were powerful, but your aura is unlike any other. You inspire me to learn and grow and be a better person."

She kissed my lips lightly, then laid her head upon my chest, pulling her leg up over mine, pressing her naked body close to my side. My arousal stirred, faint, but I was tired and knew she simply wanted to rest, nothing more. There was little sienna in her aura.

Her voice grew soft, just a breath as sleep began to claim her. "You are my rock, my home. I love you."

"And you are mine," I mumbled, kissing the top of her head.

And for the first time in what seemed like ages, I closed my eyes and found a true and tranquil rest.

CHAPTER 27

Tisera

It seemed like a lifetime, but after nearly three months my work with Prince Victor was finally done.

In that time, Eromore had sued for peace, and new borders — agreeable to both nations — had been established. Relations with Ossara had been renewed, and Victor had begun reparations with his wife and family. A true and tranquil peace — without the looming threat of war — had finally settled over Pearlia. For that I was eternally grateful.

Despite being a lifelong warrior, my soul cried out for peace. More and more I sought the joy that came from helping people. And now that I was done with the prince, I'd need to take some time and figure out what I wanted to do with my life.

To that end, I'd started taking long walks in the palace gardens to consider my future. Kel found me one day, as I sat — staring at an array of flowers, but not really seeing them — lost in thought.

"Are you well?" Kel said sitting on the bench next to me. "You've seemed distant these past few days."

I leaned into him, putting my arms around him. He embraced me, and I was comforted by those strong arms. "I want no more of war," I whispered.

"Ah... yes. I'm coming to realize that myself." He sighed heavily. "I'll be a field marshal soon, commanding the entirety of Pearlia's forces. But... I'll be working hard with our emissaries to find non-violent ways of solving our problems with other nations."

Kel was a hero now. Our fight with the Eromorn generals had become a thing of legend, but more and more Kel was the hero of the story. He alone had fought all the generals, then forced the army to flee. The rest of us played various supporting roles depending on who told the tale, but Kel was always the hero.

The queen had sought to make the most of Kel's new fame, promoting him as he'd desired. And with our nation finally at peace, he'd be here, at the palace, most of the time. He'd still be called away occasionally, but the chance of war seemed unlikely now. For that I was thankful.

I squeezed him a bit tighter and whispered, "You're in a position to influence our nation and make sure this peace lasts, but me, I don't know what I want to do yet."

The queen had offered me the role of palace guard instructor once again, but I hadn't accepted yet. I wanted to be sure before I made any big decisions. Though, one thing I had done, even before I'd finished my work with

Prince Victor was summon the Sword Skirts to the palace and resume my training with them.

After hearing about my work with them and why it was required, the queen had instituted some new laws around the freedoms of women. No more would ladies be subjugated by fathers and husbands. That meant all my ladies were free to come to the palace and train with me as they liked. And hopefully they would never *need* to use what they learned. That was work I wanted to continue, as for the rest... I still needed to figure that out.

"Maybe a walk will clear your head?" Kel asked. He rose and offered me a hand. I was no courtly lady, needing a helping hand to stand up, but I took the offered hand anyway, interlocking my fingers with his as we walked through the gardens.

The day was clear and bright with a breeze off the bay. Fall was upon us, and the heat of summer was past, but the day was still pleasantly warm. Kel's presence was reassuring, his warmth and strength comforting. It allowed me to release some of the tension in my muscles. I drew in a deep breath as we walked in silence.

"What do I want?" I asked myself.

Kel smiled down at me and didn't interrupt my musing.

All my life I'd been a warrior. All I knew was war and fighting. I couldn't be an ambassador, despite how much I desired peace. I was too blunt of speech.

What could a plain-spoken warrior-woman do in times of peace? I could be a caravan guard, but that still held the risk of fighting, even if bandits were rare these days.

I wanted to work with my ladies and empower them to feel stronger, braver, more confident. That meant sticking around here in the capital. And if I was going to be here and training them... I might as well be training palace guards as well.

I mulled it over for the rest of the walk, but by the time we'd returned to Leo's rooms I knew. I went to see the queen later that day and told her I'd accept the palace guard trainer position.

That was it.

I was set.

I had a direction and a new life and most importantly, I had my guys nearby. Though... the question still hung in the air about what Leo would do. The whole palace knew the four of us had been staying in his rooms. There were rumors aplenty. He'd have to make something official very soon.

The question was whether he would abdicate or... something else.

CHAPTER 28

Leonin

To reinforce his reunion with his wife, my brother held a second marriage to Princess Kira. It was a joyous occasion which included a formal entourage from Ossara. King Konstan himself came to see his daughter renew her vows.

Princess Anastasia looked radiant — and far older than her fourteen years — as Kira's maid of honor. Princess Helena, a solemn eleven-year-old, took her duties as flower girl *very* seriously, slowly proceeding down the aisle ensuring the bright red petals were evenly spread over the deep blue carpeting. Young Prince Wilhelm was Victor's ring bearer, though he did lose the ring temporarily, finding it again in his pocket after a short but frantic search.

Victor was resplendent in purple and gold. Kira had chosen an off-white dress, trimmed with gold and green, framed by an ermine cape. Their vows were sincere, and the kiss at the end suggested they had fully reconciled. Historians would later mark that as the night Princess Alina was conceived.

The ball held afterward was a bit wild. Everyone was more than ready to celebrate after the dark days the kingdom had faced over the summer.

There were two highlights to my night. The first was a slow and careful dance with my sister, Princess Alice, who was strong and sure, a rosy flush upon her cheeks. She couldn't stop smiling, happy and full of life. Tisi had been working with her, to try to help her regain some strength and it seemed to be working.

The second highlight was dancing with Tisi, to a merry tune, fast and lively. She stepped on my feet more times than I could count, but I didn't care. She smiled wide and wild, joyful, a delight to see. She had a new job here at the palace and her combat school for noble-women had been growing, with over twenty students now.

That night, Kel, Daz, Tisi, and I retired to our new suite in the palace. We'd moved out of my rooms to a larger suite with several bedrooms. Yet one of those rooms did have an extra-large bed and we used that one most often. We men gave ourselves to Tisi, inciting waves of euphoria, celebrating our love and unity, our brother-hood and joy.

The next day Kel was up early, now field marshal of the kingdom with many duties. The rest of us took our time rising.

Tisi was full of excited energy despite the little sleep we'd gotten.

"Today's the day!" she kept repeating. A day she'd been waiting for, for some time: the day she'd face Lord Herik.

Lady Twyra had not returned to the Sword Skirts, and Tisi worried for her. She'd vowed to face lord Herik again, and this time, she had the queen's new laws on her side.

Daz dressed in his Phorasti robes and Tisi wore armor, though now her armor sported a tabard with the royal crest on it, as the official palace trainer. I dressed in full princely regalia, and we headed out.

We took a carriage to the north-east district of the second ring of the city, where a massive estate sprawled on The Bay of Pearls. We were admitted and made certain the chamberlain understood we were here to see Lord Herik Watercrest, his father Lord Aldon Watercrest, and also Lady Twyra Watercrest.

As such we were just a little surprised when only the two men arrived.

"We apologize for the absence of Lady Twyra," Aldon Watercrest said with a haughty nonchalance. "She is not feeling well and will remain abed. What is it Your Highness wishes of me?" He spoke to me, even though I stood behind Tisi, who was clearly leading our party. The three of us formed a rough triangle with Tisi in front and Daz and I behind.

It took a moment before Lord Herik recognized Tisi and when he did, he exploded.

"You!" Herik spewed the word. "Father! This is the woman I told you about, the one who assaulted me, broke my arm, and plunged a dagger into my face!"

"Is this true?" Aldon looked from me to Tisi. "Have you brought this woman here to be punished?" he asked me.

"No, Lord Watercrest, I've brought her here to help her, and if necessary to arrest you and your son." I couldn't help a tight smile coming to my lips.

"What?" Lord Aldon laughed, indignation heavy in his superior tone.

"Enough of this. I'm going to check on Lady Twyra," Tisi said through clenched teeth. "Daz, keep them here." And she stalked right between the two men, who were both a little stunned.

"Stop her!" Herik shouted. He turned to follow her and only got one step. "What? Why can't I move?"

"Idiot." This from Aldon. "Can't you see they have a Phorasti with them? Don't struggle boy. Let them do as they will."

"But father they'll see—" Herik cut himself off.

"We'll see what?" I asked softly.

Aldon couldn't seem to decide who he was more upset at, us or his son.

He turned to me. "I am going to have a long talk with the queen about this." It was clearly a threat. He held a position of power as High Lord of the Treasury.

My smile grew.

"Yes," I said softly, stepping up to the man, who was nearly my height, but not quite. "You will." Also a threat.

"And your position as Master of the Royal Treasury will be on the line if she doesn't like what you have to say."

I'd had a long talk with my mother about all of this.

"Maybe you haven't heard, but the queen has recently issued some new laws pertaining to violence against women. Any nobleman found to be hurting his wife or daughters will lose all their standing and have their land and coffers confiscated. All confiscated land and funds will transfer to the women harmed."

I watched the horror spread on Aldon's face as I said this. I didn't know if the man had been violent himself. He had no daughters and his wife had been dead for years. But it was clear he knew of his son's proclivity to violence.

"Do we understand each other?" I asked.

The man nodded slowly, considering his words carefully before saying, "And what if I were to disown my son? Would that allow me to remain with my title and funds?" It seemed Lord Aldon was shrewd and cutthroat, giving up his son so easily.

"Perhaps..." I didn't want to make any promises. "I will let the queen make her ruling for you. Perhaps if you are contrite and make a sizable donation to the crown, that would go a long way?"

He nodded. "Understood."

Herik, however, didn't seem to understand quite yet. "My wife is mine to do with as I please! I bought her for a sizable amount, and she's defective! She hasn't conceived a single child for me!"

Aldon grimaced, realizing his son had just dug his own grave. The father shook his head and whispered to me, "Do with him as you please. He's never been that bright."

I nodded at the lord, then walked over to Herik.

"Release him," I said to Daz.

Herik stumbled, slightly off balance once free of Daz's power.

I waited for him to recover fully — I wanted this to be a fair fight — then I hit him. I landed the hit perfectly, an open-palm strike with the heel of my hand just under his nose. The man's head snapped back. He stumbled then fell on his ass. When he'd regained himself, he glared up at me, hatred in his eyes.

Herik was a beefy man, big in most dimensions, though not tall. He looked up at me, sizing me up. I don't know what he thought, but he scrambled to his feet, aiming a punch at my face. I caught his wrist and spun around behind him, locking his arm, and effectively immobilizing him.

I whispered into his ear. "You're never going to hurt anyone ever again."

He went stiff, finally understanding two things: first, he'd lost this fight, second, he'd lost everything else in his life.

"And you're lucky it's me you're fighting, not Tisera. She'd have been far less kind."

Tisi returned carrying Lady Twyra.

"I've healed her wounds," Tisi hissed, on the brink of lethal fury. "She was nearly unrecognizable. She's resting now, but..." It was clear she wanted to repay the violence which had been done to this poor noblewoman.

Aldon blanched when he saw her. The father pointed at his son. "It was all him!" he said, voice faltering.

Tisi glared at Aldon. "But it happened under your roof, and you didn't stop it. There will be consequences for that."

Aldon went even more pale and shut up after that.

Herik was put in chains and placed in a prison carriage. Twyra was laid on the soft bench of our carriage, and Tisi used a bit of her power to wake the woman as we rode to the palace.

Twyra's eyes fluttered open, and she gasped. "Master Tisera?"

"I'm here, Twyra. We've arrested Herik. He'll never hurt you again."

Twyra blinked. I didn't think she fully understood.

I helped explain things. "You're a free woman now, Twyra. You can return to your family, or if you wish, become a ward of the royal family. All of Lord Herik's estate and coffers shall transfer to you. You will want for nothing. You are free."

She wept then, tears of joy and gratitude. Tisi bundled the other woman in her arms and held her close.

And that was just the start of what would be a *very* good day.

I STOOD BEFORE MY MOTHER, ALONE, IN HER PRIVATE audience chamber.

"It seems you won't be heading to a temple after all," she said with a sigh. "You were always my quiet, obedient child, but I can see many things have changed for you. So, my son. Have you chosen your direction?"

I had.

I no longer wished to be a general, I'd found a new calling. I'd felt such a strong sense of justice after apprehending Lord Herik and freeing Lady Twyra. I wanted to help more people like that, and I knew exactly how to do it.

"The high magistrate of the city is an elderly man now. He may have many more good years in him, but I would like to study to replace him. I request an appointment as a senior reeve of the city, to help maintain order and enforce the queen's laws."

My mother's brows rose.

"I... was not expecting that at all." She cocked her head to one side. "But you are well studied in *everything*, and I have noted how your martial skills have progressed. You know the laws well and can apprehend those who break them. So... I see no fault in your request. I will not be able to make you the high magistrate when that role becomes available, for that is an elected position, but I'm sure if you prove yourself, you will achieve that goal. It is done." She smiled. "Is there anything else you require?"

"Ah, yeah..." I drew out the word. This was a bit of a harder ask. "I would like your permission to marry Tisera... in a joint union with myself, Field Marshal Drakoson, and Master-Phorasti Stormhold."

My mother sighed, lips pursed.

"*This*, I saw coming." She nodded. "I am already amending the marriage laws." Another sigh. "All my sons seek to test me, except Henry, he's perfect. The rest of you will drive me into an early grave." Then a soft smile. "I love you Leonin, and I know you love Tisera. I will allow this, but with one condition..."

CHAPTER 29

Kelric

TISI AND I HAD BEEN OUTFITTED WITH NEW ARMOR. SINCE it had never been used before today, we gleamed silver as we made our way to the great hall and the ceremony... in our honor.

We both wore the tabard of the royal house. I, as the new Field Marshal for all of Pearlia, and she as the official trainer of the palace guards. Daz was with us too, resplendent in his Phorasti robes.

There were shouts and cries of joy and merriment as we made our way down the long central aisle of the great hall to stand before the queen.

She rose and spoke, her voice raised to reach all corners of the large room.

"You three have shown exceptional courage and bravery in protecting our kingdom, even when we did not treat you well. For that you have our eternal thanks, and I bestow upon you the titles and ranks as follows. Please kneel."

The three of us knelt as the queen was handed a slender longsword, an ornamental weapon, which she held with ease.

She stood before me, tapping my left shoulder with the dulled blade. "Kelric Drakoson, I bestow upon you the title of Earl of the Ward." It was a mostly superfluous title. It meant I had no land holdings and was a "ward" of the Crown.

The queen moved the blade over to tap my right shoulder. "You have already been raised to the rank of Field Marshal but shall henceforth be known also as Knight-Captain of the Realm and Lord General of the Queen's Armies." She removed the blade and said: "Arise Lord Drakoson."

I rose as a cheer went up through the hall.

The queen moved to Tisi, laying the sword on her left shoulder. "Tisera Halvensdaughter, I bestow upon you, the title of Earl of the Ward."

The crowd murmured at this. No woman had ever been given the title of earl before. It hadn't been possible, women had been an extension of their husbands. Yet with the new laws the queen had implemented, all of that had changed.

Tisi would be the first female Earl in Pearlia.

The queen tapped her right shoulder and continued. "You have proven yourself capable again and again and are currently the trainer of the palace guard. I add to that, the rank of Knight-Lieutenant of the Realm and Lord Captain of the Queen's Armies."

The queen had insisted that if we were all to marry her son, we needed titles and ranks. Tisi hadn't wanted a rank in the Queen's Army, since that meant she might be called to war again. But the queen had quieted those fears before this ceremony. The title was a formality only. It would not require any active military service.

The queen removed the blade and announced, "Arise Lady Halvensdaughter."

Tisi rose, and an even larger cheer rose up from those around the hall, a distinctly feminine cheer if my ears didn't deceive me. Tisi would turn this kingdom on its head. In truth... she already had.

The queen moved to Daz, laying the blade on his left shoulder.

"Dazar Stormhold Halvenson, I bestow upon you the title of Earl of the Ward." She moved her sword to his right shoulder. "From hence force you shall be known as Friend of the Crown and shown respect and courtesy in all courts of the realm." She removed the blade: "Arise, Lord Stormhold."

Daz rose and this time there was some confused cheering. "Friend of the Crown" was a new title and not many people knew what it meant. Mostly, it had come from Daz's insistence not to have a military title.

The three of us turned and raised a hand to the assembled lords and ladies. Another cheer went up.

That was it. We were officially nobility now. I'd never thought it possible. But when you're going to joint-marry the same woman as a prince, apparently it becomes possible.

The marriage itself, despite being an official court function, was not a public affair. It was held in the queen's private audience chamber.

Tisi, of course, didn't wear a dress. She wore her dress uniform as a newly minted Knight-Lieutenant and Lord Captain. It broke every protocol, but that was just an average day for the woman I loved.

I wore my uniform. Leo was dressed in his prince's regalia, and Daz wore his Phorasti robes.

New vows had to be written, of course. We all vowed our love and fidelity to each other, a lasting bond uniting us all. Then we all kissed the bride and there was a small gathering of the royal family and close friends.

Then came the wedding night.

Luckily, the practice of an audience watching the consummation of a royal marriage had long passed, otherwise, that group would have learned a thing or two. We were *very* vigorous in our affections and exposed Tisi to new heights of screaming bliss.

We ordered a new mattress the next day.

A few days later, Tisi and I had a moment alone, walking through the palace on the way to our various duties: me to a meeting with the generals, her to a training session with her ladies.

"Could you ever have imagined this would be your life?" I asked, looking around at the palace halls and the busy servants.

She laughed, a light and free sound, which made my heart take flight with joy.

"Nope, couldn't have imagined any of this. If my father had told me that someday I'd be a noblewoman, the first Lady-Earl, and captain-trainer of the palace guard, who also trains noblewomen in combat, I'd have wondered what strange drug he was smoking. It's all a little... unbelievable, isn't it?"

That's where she was wrong.

"No, Tisi, it isn't. You've never been anything but loyal to this kingdom. You help people at every turn and do far more than is asked of you. This may seem like a fairy-tale, but knowing you the way I do, I can see every step that led you here. You deserve all of this."

She blushed at that.

"Thank you, Kel," she said sincerely. Then she laughed. "And our past selves would have been horrified to know we got married."

"With two other men in the mix as well," I added.

"And one of them a prince."

"The other a Phorasti!"

We both laughed at the seeming absurdity of that. "We've come a long way, you and I," I said softly, arm around her shoulder. "Apprentices together, then comrades in arms. Then lovers, then enemies, then..."

"Married," she finished.

I hugged her close beside me as we walked.

She stopped suddenly and I halted with her. She turned to me, lowering her voice. "I love you, Kel. Thank you for... your strength and the warm comfort of your arms. You may not be a prince or a wizard, but you're all man and all mine and I love you."

She drew my face down to hers in a soft but heartfelt kiss.

When I drew back, I said, in an equally sincere tone, "You may not be what other men think of as 'all woman,' but you're the woman I want. I love you, Tisi, I always have and always will."

And this time when we kissed... well, we were both late for our appointments.

CHAPTER 30

TISERA

I COULDN'T CONTAIN MY EXCITEMENT. TODAY THE FIRST class of women would graduate from the Sword Skirts.

In truth, they were only graduating their "first level" of training. They'd be continuing to train with me at a more advanced level, while helping to train those below them. And I'd need their help. There were now almost fifty women — and even a few young men — in my school, including all three of Prince Victor's children — Anastasia, Helena, and Wilhelm — and Prince Henry's son, Alfran as well.

It wasn't a large graduating class, only four students.

Lady Emarra would advance, that didn't surprise me. She'd been razor focused on her training. Even when I'd not been there to train them, she'd practiced daily and helped some of her friends as well.

Avela, the shepherdess who tended my cottage with the aging Shorine, would also graduate. She had joined a bit later but had taken to the training with ease. She had a natural grace and just a bit of a chip on her shoulder. A nasty combination, but it made her all the more determined.

The last two were Lady Sinda Rosewood and Lady Willow Highcastle. Both of them had been in the original group with Emarra but had not had her drive. Still, they had done well and had a firm grasp of the basic skills. Lady Highcastle was still a bit tentative, but I hoped that becoming a teacher might help her gain confidence.

I'd settled on colored sashes to help denote the ranks of my students. Beginners would have no sash. My four students today were graduating to a yellow sash. From there, they could move up to an expert level orange sash. And if they got to my level, a master, they'd earn a red sash.

I wore my bright red sash with pride. Daz had said the color was perfect for me, since my aura was mostly red. I didn't much care if it looked good or not.

But... it did look good.

I stood on a raised platform in the courtyard of the palace and called up the four, one by one presenting them with their sashes. They tied them around their waists, each to their own tastes and style and stood before the others.

I hadn't really thought the sashes would be much of an incentive to move up in the ranks, but the amount of murmuring and pointing made me think some of these young women might work a little harder, just to earn a pretty sash.

Women were strange.

The next part of the ceremony was a special skills presentation. I wanted to highlight some of the other students who — though their overall progress wasn't at a level to move on — did possess some exceptional skills in one area.

The first was Lady Twyra.

She had applied herself with vigor to her training and would have moved on if she hadn't missed several months. She still had a few basic areas to learn, but her skill with a bow was unmatched. She demonstrated by having me throw targets — a circular wooden frame with colored fabric stretched over it — up into the air at different speeds and intervals. She pierced every single one. I presented her with an award for archery skills.

Next was the precocious Princess Anastasia. She had been practicing relentlessly with throwing knives and daggers. Three targets had been set up for her. She threw light darts at the first, a weapon I hadn't even taught her. She'd learned it all on her own, using a special throwing style. The three darts landed clustered around the bull's eye.

The crowd cheered.

On the second target, the princess demonstrated her skill with small light knives designed to be thrown. She threw three knives so fast it took everyone a moment to realize she was done. Moreover, her accuracy was spot on.

For the last target, she had me throw a larger parrying dagger first. I hit about a hand-span off the center, up and to the right. Her goal was to get her three daggers closer to center than mine. These heavier weapons took a bit longer to throw, requiring a bit more aim and effort. The first hit beside mine, but still slightly closer to center. For the second, she over-compensated a little and hit down and to the left, about as far away as mine was. The third... hit dead center.

The crowd went wild.

Anastasia beamed and bowed.

I gave her the unique "Deadliest Royal" award and joked that she was a better warrior than her father or uncles. She clutched her placard with pride. Some girls liked dolls, others liked throwing knives. Anastasia was *my* kind of woman.

That was it for the day's festivities. We proceeded with lessons as usual, with my newly appointed advanced students helping out. Afterward, I walked with Avela back to my cottage in the second ring of the city. It had been a while since I'd been back, and I had a few things I wanted to gather. I also had some good news for Shorine and Avela, but I wanted to wait and tell them both together.

Walking down the laneway toward the small cabin where I'd been raised, I found myself overwhelmed with memories.

Leo and I had met — and an awkward meeting it had been — at the end of the lane.

And... later, we'd had our first *intimate moment* behind a large tree just down the lane a little.

I had begun my school on these lawns.

I'd been introduced to Prince Victor by Kel — whom I despised at the time — in this yard.

Many — so very many — good times had been had in my baths in the juniper grove.

And for the longest time Daz and I had lived in the cottage, together but apart, until he'd finally told me how he felt.

"Please, can you find Shorine and bring her?" I asked Avela. "I have something I'd like to tell you both."

Avela smiled and nodded, running off.

I gathered the last of my things, cleaning out my room. Daz had been by a few days earlier to do the same with his room. Then I waited in the kitchen. I was over-whelmed with memories of the amazing meals Daz had prepared for me here. He might have been a powerful mystic, but he'd always been so willing to do mundane work: cooking and cleaning. He was an amazing man, and I was very glad I'd been able to see all sides of him.

Avela returned with Shorine. The old woman had worked here since before I was born, yet still seemed healthy and strong.

"As you may have guessed," I began with a bitter-sweet smile, "Daz and I are moving out." I drew in a long breath, still not quite believing it.

"I'm sure you've seen us gathering our things. We have a suite at the palace now and want to be there, close to Kel and Prince Leo. But... this place is still my home, and I would never sell it."

Here came the fun part. "I know you two will take good care of everything here and I — well, Daz and I — want *you two* to have the cottage."

I grinned at the stunned surprise on their two faces.

I continued with joy. "There's no need for you to remain in that small house if this place is empty. Please come and live here. A reward for all your years of work. I'm leaving all of this to you. It will be yours to do with as you please. Oh... and I have a steady income from the crown now, so the taxes will be paid, and you'll have a monthly income of two slips of silver... each." It was far more than they'd ever been paid before.

"What do you think?" I asked. I'd watched their faces display a mix of awe, gratitude, and joy.

Shorine came and embraced me.

"Thank you, my dear. You... you are your father's daughter," she whispered to me. That comment flooded me with warmth and a sorrowful joy. I had modeled my life on that of my father's. For her to say this... was a huge affirmation of everything I'd worked toward. I was overcome with pride and recognition.

"Thank you," I said, hugging her back, tears of joy in my eyes.

Avela came over and put her arms around us both. "Thank you, Tisi."

"You two deserve this," I said, sniffing back my emotions.

We exchanged a few other kind words, then said our good-byes and Avela escorted me back down the lane. "I... wanted to get you alone to say: I'm glad that you and Daz figured things out between you. It was exhausting watching you at times."

I laughed at that. "I bet it was. I was so oblivious."

"Yes, you were." She laughed with me. "And I'm glad

you've found those others as well. I know they'll make you happy."

I embraced her. "Now, it's your turn," I said. "Find someone who makes *you* happy."

Avela giggled. "Hadn't you noticed?"

Noticed? "No, what? Have you found someone?" I was suddenly ever-so-curious.

"I have." She lowered her voice to a conspiratorial tone. "Lady Willow Highcastle and I have been seeing each other."

"Lady...?" I blinked.

No, I hadn't noticed that at all! But now that I thought of it, Avela's choice made sense. She'd had a rough life before she'd come to be with me, and Lady Willow was soft and kind and gentle.

I smiled. "I'm happy for you." Then I laughed a little. "You're going to shake up the nobility as much as I did."

"I hope so," she said with a wide grin.

We parted and I found myself smiling all the way back to the palace. Not only from Avela's happy news, but I had some happy news of my own for the guys.

My guys — my wonderful, loving guys — were all in the suite when I returned.

Good.

"I have an announcement," I said.

The three of them gathered in the main living area. Daz and Leo sat on a long couch, while Kel leaned his bulk on the back of it.

They waited, love in their eyes, as I figured out how to tell them my news.

"Now that I have better control over my powers, I can

feel a song inside me all the time. It is my anthem, a tune that is mine and mine alone. It is wonderful and strong and beautiful—"

"Like you," Leo cut in quickly.

I smiled.

"That hadn't been where I was going but thank you. No, what I wanted to say was that, over the last few days, I've noticed something. There is a new song inside me, a different song. It took me far too long to figure out what that meant. But I know now, I'm certain..."

I met each of their gazes: Kel's dark pools of sable, Daz's warm caramel-gold, and Leo's soft and peaceful sea-green.

"I'm pregnant," I said. "You are going to be fathers."

I watched that sink in.

Then all three of them were up, encircling me and holding me close.

"Tisi, that's wonderful!" Leo said, elated.

"I'm... going to be a father..." Kel's tone was just a little stunned.

"How do *you* feel about this?" Daz asked me.

That was a hard question to answer.

"I'm... I never thought I'd be a mother. I was a warrior for so long, pregnancy and fighting don't really go hand in hand. But my life is more peaceful now and... I want a child... or two... or three." I looked at them all intently as they got my meaning.

The silly grins on their faces made me laugh, feeling light and at ease.

"Needless to say, I'm excited and surprised... well, no, not really surprised, given how virile and potent you three are. If anything I'm surprised it's taken this long. Mostly I'm still figuring this out, but I know I want this child and I'll love this child."

I was glad none of them had asked whose it was. They didn't seem to care. They would be co-fathers to this child no matter who the biological father was.

But *I* knew.

I could tell from the child's song that my first child would be a little prince or princess, since Leo hadn't abdicated his position.

"We should celebrate!" Leo said, excited.

"Want to try for twins?" Kel chuckled, low and deep, his insinuation clear.

"I'm pretty sure it doesn't work that way," I added.

"I was thinking more like a nice dinner," Leo said.

I looked over at Daz. He had his head cocked the way he did when he was thinking intently or using his powers in a very delicate way.

"What?" I asked him.

"It's a girl," he whispered to me. "I can feel her aura now that I'm looking for it. And... she'll be even stronger than you are, I know it."

A girl...?

My eyes welled with tears.

"Thank you," I whispered to Daz. I pulled him close and kissed him. I then interrupted Leo and Kel's playful argument — over how we'd celebrate — to kiss them both.

"Thank you all, for... everything!" I said, overwhelmed with joy. "I love you all, and a part of me still can't believe you all love me in return. I'm so lucky. I couldn't ask for three better men."

They all beamed and moved in close once again, surrounding me with their warmth and devotion.

Here, in the arms of these three men was where I belonged. They were my home, my life, my family. There was no doubt in my mind that I was worthy of their love, all of their love, and I couldn't be happier.

GLOSSARY

CURRENCY

- ¼ bronze piece – "A Quarter"
- ½ bronze piece – "A Cut Piece"
- bronze coin – "A Sail"
- small silver bar – "A Slip" (=10 sails)
- large silver bar – "A Strip" (=10 slips)
- gold coin – "A Royal" (=50 strips)
- gold bar – "A Bar" (=50 royals)

PLACES OF NOTE

Aestria

Eastern Continent

(Ancient Aestria / Aestrian Empire)

A massive empire over the entire continent. Over

the last thousand years the empire has been in decline – devouring natural resources – many regions starving while the larger cities and the capital grew more opulent. There were many revolts and uprisings. About two hundred years ago, a merchant ship, blown off course in a storm, found its way to Valterra. This began a mass exodus of ships and settlers which sought to leave the empire and settle new kingdoms. Aestria sent merchants and workers to harvest the natural resources of Valterra to return to Aestria, but most of them simply stayed and few resources returned to the empire. Over the last century and a half, the empire fractured into small city-stakes and kingdoms, stuck in the old ways.

The Narrow Sea

Separates Aestria from Valterra

Despite its name it isn't a quick trip across – from the narrowest point it takes about two days to cross, but few take that route as it's far to the north and the strong winds which make the trip quick also make it treacherous. Most sail calmer waters to the south, where it takes anywhere from four to six days to cross in calm weather. Pearlia to Therist (Aestrian city) takes about three to five days depending on winds.

Valterra

Western Continent

Inhabited by Dathi and Usovi peoples in the south and barbarian tribes, north of the Valterran Mountains. Roughly two hundred years ago peoples from Aestria came across the Narrow Sea to settle here.

Usura / Usurn Wilds / The Wildlands
South of continent – a desert and badlands, farther south is a dense jungle. Home of Usovi People. Some remain nomadic, others settled areas of rich resources.

Dathi Lands
The lush mid-region of Valterra, now mostly settled by Aestrians. Dathi were a nomadic people, most of whom were friendly and many settled among the Aestrian cities. A few, purists, stuck to the old ways. The Purists began a war of genocide to eradicate all "impure" mixed-blood Dathi, but the mixed-blood were aided by the aestrian cities and quickly overwhelmed the Purists.

Pearlia
Oldest of the Aestrian settled kingdoms in Valterra, sitting along the Pearline River on the Narrow Sea. The river had been known as the Hanoea River by the Dathi previously. Possesses a

deep protected harbor, abundant with oysters and pearls (hence the name)

Three Rings:

The Inner Ring / Old City – where the first settlers landed and built original city.

The Second Ring – originally the park-like estates of noblemen outside of the city. A second wall was built to protect these lands.

Third Ring – the peasant community outside the wall, taller buildings over narrow alleys with few wide roads. A third wall was erected to protect this area, completed roughly twenty years ago

Outside the city slums nestle close to the wall and farther out a caravansary and market of trade goods has sprung up, since many foreign merchants cannot gain access to the city. New Nobles estates have been built outside the walls along the river

Eromore

On the Erovan River, in the North of Valterra, where lands are not as fertile as Pearlia. Have spent generations building their armies to protect from invading barbarians in the north. Recent turned their attentions south to Pearlia.

Vestrea – a southern province of Eromore – war between Eromore and Pearlia divided it up – the bulk staying in Eromore, with the capital and some surrounding southern lands going to Pearlia.

Ossara

Further up the Pearline River on Lake Ostri (Originally named Aester Lake by the new residents, but the Dathi called it Oenin. The names combined over time). Proud peoples – the lake is large, but they are landlocked and cannot get to sea without going through Pearlia – have always had a decent relationship with Pearlia.

Rolvan

South of Pearlia on the edge of the dessert and wilds. Rolvan is a trade city, where Dathi and Usovi come from the west and south to exchange wares. Aestrian, Dathi, and Usovi alike often venture into the dessert and wilds to find ancient (sometimes mystical) artifacts of a lost civilization.

Myrna

Farthest west kingdom, at the edge of settled lands in Valterra, a small kingdom, growing slowly. Trade with still nomadic Dathi who move through the western woods

PEARLIAN ROYAL FAMILY

King Edward Pearlece
   Died 7 years ago

Queen Helena Pearlece
   Ruling

Prince Victor Pearlece
    Heir apparent
    Married to Princess Kira of Ossara
    Daughter Princess Anastasia (14)
    Daughter Princess Helena (11)
    Son Prince Wilhelm (8)

Princess Beatrice / Queen Beatrice
    Married to King Tharin of Rolvan
    Son Prince Fredrin (16)
    Son Prince Edric (14)
    Son Prince Nikalas (11)

Princess Alice Pearlece
    Never married

Prince Henry Pearlece
    Married to Lady Miraline Highwald
    Son Prince Alfran (8)
    Daughter Princess Gwendolyn (4)

Prince Leonin Pearlece
    Married to Lady Theodora of Vestrea who died 4 years ago
    No children

GODS AND RELIGIONS

Aestrian Deities

Aestric

   Father Deity – Ruler of the Heavens
   God of Rulership, Law, Justice

Assa

   Mother Deity – Queen of the Heavens
   Goddess of Creation, Rebirth, Mercy

Brovos

   God of War and Victory

Halea

   Goddess of Love, Sensuality, Fertility

Wisteri

   Goddess of Knowledge and Learning

Olerin

   God of Cultivation, Agriculture, Husbandry

Lenara

   Goddess of Nature, Wild Animals, Freedom

Dathi & Usovi Deities

Moena

   The Creator
   Neither / Both Genders
   Took a part of themselves to create the world

The Children of Moena
The Dathi and Usovi believe all the peoples of the world are the children of Moena. Moena also created Great Spirits (demi-gods) to help rule over specific domains:

Suoma – The Land
    "God" of Protection, Strength

Evos – The Great Waters (seas/lakes)
    "Goddess" of Love, Fertility

Kuso – The Lesser Waters (rivers and streams)
    Son of Suoma and Evos
    "God" of Travel, Journeys, Trade

Ohan – Forests and Jungles
    Son of Suoma and Evos
    "God" of Wildlife

Apa – The Sun
    "God" of Knowledge

Kihuana – The Sky (sometimes light, sometimes dark & stary)
    "Goddess" of Secrets

Tawandi – The Wind & Storm
    Daughter of Apa and Kihuana
    "Goddess" of Fate, Change

Nalo – Fire

Son of Ohan and Tawandi (lightning striking trees)
"God" of Chance, Desire

Datha – The Great Wolf
    Dathi peoples are named after him

Uso – The Great Bear
    Usovi peoples are named after her

OTHER BOOKS BY CLARA WILS